T0286025

Praise for

THE RELUCTANT DISCIPLE

"If you are looking for meaning in this world, look no further than *The Reluctant Disciple*. Robin takes you on a journey to help you realize that God places you where you are for a reason. Enjoy the journey, find a quiet place, and listen to your heart as you read this life-changing book."

—GRANT MOISE, CEO of the DallasNews Corp., president and publisher of *The Dallas Morning News*

"Robin is a respected executive coach, accomplished author, and great leader. His life story, mirrored in *The Reluctant Disciple,* is one of healing, hope, and, ultimately, heroism. Powerful and accessible, *The Reluctant Disciple* shares a simple message— God is with us in our toughest times."

—CLARK HUNT, chairman and CEO of the NFL's Kansas City Chiefs

The
RELUCTANT
DISCIPLE

A PARABLE ABOUT
RECONCILING FAITH & BUSINESS

AN UNEXPECTED JOURNEY OF GOD'S PROVISION

ROBIN POU

GREENLEAF
BOOK GROUP PRESS

Published by Greenleaf Book Group Press
Austin, Texas
www.gbgpress.com

Distributed by Greenleaf Book Group

For ordering information or special discounts for bulk purchases, please contact
Greenleaf Book Group at PO Box 91869, Austin, TX 78709, 512.891.6100.

Design and composition by Greenleaf Book Group
Cover design by Greenleaf Book Group
Cover Image from Adobe Stock

Publisher's Cataloging-in-Publication data is available.

Print ISBN: 979-8-88645-171-9

eBook ISBN: 979-8-88645-172-6

To offset the number of trees consumed in the printing of our books, Greenleaf
donates a portion of the proceeds from each printing to the Arbor Day Foundation.
Greenleaf Book Group has replaced over 50,000 trees since 2007.

Printed in the United States of America on acid-free paper

24 25 26 27 28 29 30 31   10 9 8 7 6 5 4 3 2 1

First Edition

My sweet wife, Karen—you are one of the most joyful and inspiring people I know. I am excited to see what God has in store for us in the years ahead. TMISB!

CONTENTS

Author's Note ix

Saturday 1

    1: Flying Private 3

    2: The Mountaintop Experience 11

    3: Dashing through the Snow 23

    4: Pinned Down 29

Sunday 35

    5: Jim and Mary 37

    6: Once a Boy Scout, Always a Boy Scout 45

Monday 51

    7: Like Old Friends 53

    8: Bible Study 59

    9: The Struggle Is Real 65

Tuesday 71

    10: Déjà Vu 73

    11: Mimi 79

    12: Not Guaranteed 85

Wednesday 95

    13: Close to God 97

    14: In the Game 105

    15: Give God the Glory 115

Thursday   123

16: Missing the Turnoff   125

17: Sucker Punched   129

18: Good or Bad?   137

Friday   141

19: Hallelujah   143

20: Let God Defend You   149

21: Breakfast with a Side of Forgiveness   153

Saturday   159

22: Coffee and a Calling   161

23: Good Luck Charm   167

24: Fathers' Blessings   169

25: Grace and Mercy   175

26: The Favor   179

Sunday   183

27: The Crash Site   185

28: A Gift and Goodbye   189

29: Homebound   193

About the Author   197

AUTHOR'S NOTE

The Reluctant Disciple is a parable inspired by harrowing true events that I experienced during the summer of 2007. After being unexpectedly fired from my job by a formerly trusted cofounder, I was stunned and grappling with my next professional move.

My good friend Sharla insisted that I go to Kenya, Africa, on a short-term mission trip with our local church, Highland Park Presbyterian Church. The purpose of the trip was to support a clean water initiative in Njuthine, a small village at the base of Mount Kenya approximately five hours from Nairobi—the home village of one of our church pastors.

I reluctantly agreed to the trip all the while questioning my own purpose for the journey. Perhaps I might be able to do some good even amid professional turmoil. On the first night after leaving the small village in the remote Kenyan bush, my group's van was stopped by violent thugs armed with guns and machetes. All thirteen missionaries were taken against our will into the darkness. The captors' brutality turned the goodwill trip into a life-or-death experience.

As I lay face down in a ditch by the side of the road, sensing a catastrophic end to the ordeal, I unexpectedly discovered the answer to the ultimate question: *What's my purpose?*

A miraculous turn of events led to our eventual escape and opened my eyes to the true meaning of grace. I left reluctance behind. I died in the ditch that day only to live again with a compulsion to pursue a fully integrated, faith-filled life. This deepened faith in a living and active God entirely changed my perspective on my role in the marketplace and the definition of "success." I have been led to share my experiences with those who wrestle with reconciling their faith and business endeavors.

Shortly after my return, I founded a leadership development firm dedicated to helping executives and top leaders maximize their full potential and impact with their teams and in their industries. Before my trip to Kenya, I was known for building businesses. Now I build up leaders who build businesses positioned to impact the market in a significant way—my God-given life's work.

As you read about Pete's journey, it is my hope and prayer that you find encouragement and clarity in the midst of any challenges you may be facing.

SATURDAY

1

FLYING PRIVATE

STEPPING OUT OF A CADILLAC ESCALADE at Love Field's Signature Flight Terminal, Peter Christiansen carried the tattered briefcase his father had given him almost twenty years ago at his high school graduation. This trusty satchel had come in handy through every up and down that life had thrown his way. It was his good luck charm. He even called it Lady Luck. He was about to be ushered into a private jet, in which he would be flown to New Mexico to sign the biggest deal of his sixteen-year career as an up-and-coming home builder.

Peter had never flown private, unlike many of his clients—and potential clients. Although he'd built his business from the ground up, into a thriving firm, he was still on the outside of the Dallas home builder market. He still had a long way to go as he continued to break into the wealthier enclaves of the city. He longed for his little start-up to reach what he believed to be its true potential. One day, it would be the number-one home builder in the city.

He stepped onto the tarmac, and the smiling flight attendant, who looked like she spent her Sundays cheering for the Dallas Cowboys, guided him toward the short flight of steps up to the entrance to the Bombardier. *Just three little steps to my destiny*, he thought.

Flying private. If Peter had heard that phrase once, he had heard it a thousand times from the lips of his new friends. *We're going skiing, and we're flying private. We're going to the Super Bowl, and we're flying private. We're going to Dad's birthday party, and we're flying private.* It seemed that the dividing line between those who hired Peter's firm and those who didn't was whether they could afford to fly private. Those wealthy enough to do so might have favored Peter with an interview, but they never gave him the deal.

As he stepped through the doorway, Peter realized that no one else was in the passenger compartment. This jet was all for him for the short hop to Taos. As his eyes adjusted to the soft light of the interior, he studied the impeccable leather seats, the plush carpeting, the glossy wood table and chairs. Peter could tell at a glance that they were the same quality of finishes he hoped to adorn the houses of his future überwealthy clients' homes with.

Whoever heard of a full-size sofa in an airplane? he thought as he lowered himself into one of the swivel chairs. He tried to look comfortable, like he belonged in this chair that probably cost more than his first car. But his eyes lit up like those of a ten-year-old boy on Christmas morning, hopeful he would finally get the coveted Red Ryder BB gun.

"First time flying private?" the flight attendant asked sweetly.

"Is it that obvious?" Peter asked, chagrined, as he felt his cheeks turning red.

"I won't tell anyone," she replied, grinning. "Everybody feels that way the first time. Don't be embarrassed. Your secret is safe with me. Champagne?"

Beer was more to his taste. Champagne always struck him as reserved for the more sophisticated set, the kind whose pinky stuck out ever so slightly when attempting to drink from the ridiculously tall glass. He'd never seen his dad, a Vietnam vet, drink champagne. A six pack of Budweiser though? Definitely. The King of Beers. Plus, champagne gave Peter a headache. But, when in Rome.

"Um . . . sure. I mean, yes, please." He might not have been raised with money, but his mother had taught him how to behave. She always said, "Peter Jonathan Christensen, I just have two words for you: Behave!" He always rolled his eyes at her play on words. He had stuck to them pretty well, but he wondered where it had actually gotten him.

At that moment, the pilot stepped out of the cockpit. His presence startled Peter as if he had done something wrong. What flying private etiquette had he failed to follow?

The pilot was exactly as Peter would have expected, like he had been sent over by Central Casting. He was tall, silver-haired, and had the ramrod-straight bearing of someone who was clearly ex-military.

"Good morning, Mr. Christensen," he said. "I'll be taking you over to Taos today. We're expecting a storm later on, but we'll have you on the ground well before it arrives."

In the movies, private pilots always said they were flying "over to" the destination—no big deal, as if they were just heading over to the 7-Eleven for some snacks and a copy of the Sunday edition of the *Dallas Morning News*.

"Are we good to go?" the pilot asked.

"Yes, sir," Peter offered, hearing his mom's voice in his ear. *Why did I say that? I'm not a child.* He gave the pilot a thumbs-up, immediately wondering if that looked geeky. Yep. That was geeky.

The pilot nodded and forced a smile, as if to confirm—*clearly a rookie*—and then made his way back into the cockpit.

Peter felt a twinge of uneasiness, the way he always did when some subtle signal emphasized the differences between the luxuries his clients and neighbors took for granted and the working-class life he had known growing up. Would he *ever* feel like he belonged? He sighed. Suddenly, the powerful engines roared to life, and Peter was on his way. As the jet slowly made its way down the runway, he sat back, accepted the glass of champagne from the flight attendant, and asked himself how on earth he had gotten here.

The jet took off with a jolt almost immediately after heading down the runway, stirring Peter's stomach even further. Attempting to return to elation, he marveled at the fact that there weren't a dozen planes ahead of his.

He was first. He wondered whether flying private meant you got to jump to the start of the line. Suddenly he was airborne.

Trying to settle in, Peter felt the seat was a bit snug, so he pulled his phone and wallet out of his pocket and slipped them into his satchel to make some room. He had always been big for his age, and although he had the finesse to play skill positions, every football coach he'd ever had had made him a guard. People used to say that you just couldn't get past Peter with a football; maybe it was that he played with a chip on both shoulders. Peter was a workhorse, not a show pony. He was reliable. Making room for others, that was his role—comfortable for him but often overlooked.

Back in high school, the future was something too vague to think seriously about, and many from his old neighborhood didn't have a lot of vision beyond their front sidewalks. What would they do when they grew up? Whatever their fathers had done. And if their fathers hadn't done anything? Then neither would they. Football helped Peter channel his physical prowess into a meaningful pathway on the field and, later, in life. If not for the sport, Peter well knew he probably would have stayed in his neighborhood and nothing good would ever have happened in his life.

The turning point came when his high school football team played an away game against Highland Park, an elite high school in the prestigious Park Cities neighborhood in the middle of Dallas. The locker room at his high school in Mesquite was so dilapidated that most of the players preferred to dress and shower at home and come to games in their pads and cleats rather than face whatever fungus might be lurking in the showers. Highland Park was on another planet by comparison. The visitors' locker room was magnificent, with spotless tiled showers, leather chairs, and every amenity a high school football player could dream of. The cheerleaders were beyond gorgeous too.

As Mesquite's embarrassingly rickety school bus took the boys into and out of the lavish neighborhood, Peter could not help but notice the houses on every block, each lawn perfectly manicured. It wasn't so much that each house was massive—they were—but they were also absolutely stunning. To Peter, they were works of art. They weren't rows of cookie-cutter houses stamped out quickly and forgotten. These were phenomenal, intentionally crafted structures. Some creator had thought of every detail for a specific purpose. Each was unique, with its own special attributes. He wondered whether the people who lived in them appreciated the magnificence as much as he did merely seeing the outside.

Now they were reaching cruising altitude, and the flight attendant asked Peter if he was ready for dinner.

"I can offer you filet or lobster or both," she said.

Peter tried to act as if choosing between filet and lobster were an everyday occurrence for him. He never ate lobster and he had not even had a real steak until his first pregame meal as a football student during his first year of college.

"I'd like both, please," he said, grinning sheepishly at the flight attendant. "If it's not too much trouble."

She gave Peter a smile that suggested that her whole life had led up to the moment where she could offer him surf and turf. She retrieved the champagne bottle. He happily allowed her to refill his glass, hoping it would calm his nerves.

Peter put his worry to work by placing his arms behind his head and studying the cabin, locking every detail into his memory bank to make it all real. He couldn't wait to describe it to his wife—formerly one of those cheerleaders from Highland Park. In fact, his wife had set this deal into motion to begin with; she and the prospective client had known each other growing up.

Peter winced a bit; he didn't like relying on anyone—even his wife. It wouldn't truly be his success if he had to be carried along the way. He was a pull-yourself-up-by-your-bootstraps kind of guy. His dad used to say, "You can't rely on anyone but yourself in this world." But a little helping hand is what family was for, right? He would design and build the Taos house himself, after all, and then Peter would be on an entirely different professional level. Maybe he and his family would be able to fly private any day of the week.

Of course, if the deal didn't come through . . . Peter's business had stalled as of late, and he couldn't quite figure out why. Attempting to break into the luxury housing market was tough. One by one, he'd thought he'd had the sale sewn up, only to discover in a roundabout way—no one ever seemed to have the decency to tell him face-to-face—that he'd lost out to another builder. The commission on the Taos house would more than erase his current cash flow worries. He just needed that signature.

This recent run of bad luck only reinforced Peter's belief that he was relegated to be an outsider, no matter how much he tried. The message he got felt like the classic "You are not from here, kid, so you aren't going to get the work." This was no glass ceiling; it was impenetrable steel. Maybe things would be different this time, with his wife—who *was* an insider in this world—having greased the skids.

Because of Peter's size, he had had no problem finding construction work during the summers, even in high school. The owner of one of the construction companies he worked for had seen Peter play against Highland Park. This University of Texas alum had grown up in Mesquite himself, was a big booster of the football team, and casually described Peter's abilities, and his smarts, to the head football coach at UT Austin. Peter had never even imagined he would go to college, but he was suddenly on his way, only two hundred miles from home but a world away. Little did he know at the time that his benefactor would eventually be his father-in-law.

His degree in engineering and a natural flair for design, along with a chance introduction at a recruiting event, paved the way for a role as a junior associate at the offices of Hunsacker, Inc. The firm was owned by Digby Hunsacker, who, for years, had been the most prestigious designer and builder of houses in Dallas.

As Peter sipped his champagne and stared out the window at West Texas, he could see clouds forming on the horizon. Peter was hopeful that the pilot was right; his weather app said that the storm wouldn't roll into Taos until two or three in the morning.

The thought crossed his mind to pray that the storm would hold off. But that seemed silly. "Hey, God, I have a huge deal I have to get done so I can pay my bills, preserve my fledgling reputation, and satisfy my yearslong ambition to be somebody in this world. Can you please . . . pretty please hold this storm off?"

First, Peter thought, *does it even work like that? Second, how selfish my request seems, given the starving kids around the world. Third, does God even care about my deal?*

Anyway, the pilot had said they'd be back on the ground before the storm hit, so it didn't really matter. The timing was perfect.

Let it *snow if it's going to snow*, Peter thought.

Peter cut into the filet, which was as tender and juicy as anything he had ever eaten in his life. How could they serve such amazing food on a plane? Even when he got upgraded to first class on a commercial flight, the food was good but not great. This whole flying private thing was something he could definitely get used to, he decided. After he signed the deal today, maybe he'd get the chance.

His new client, Edward J. Robinson III, was throwing an early holiday party with all of his hedge fund buddies to celebrate the closing of his newest billion-dollar fund. He had asked Peter to come ink the Taos deal and to do the first official site visit for the project before winter truly set in. Peter was hopeful he might also get to meet a couple of prospects with practically unlimited resources and the desire to build houses—second, third, or fourth houses—anywhere from Denver to Dubai.

Not bad for a kid from the other side of the tracks. Peter savored his dinner and turned down a third glass of champagne. He wanted to be on his game for his meeting, without anything slowing him down.

Nothing can stop me now, Peter thought.

He glanced out the window and noticed that the clouds were thickening. Certainly, no cloud cover could come in the way of what he felt was his destiny. He shrugged it off. He was flying higher than he'd ever flown in his life—flying private, even—and things were about to get even better.

2

THE MOUNTAINTOP EXPERIENCE

PETER LANDED AT THE PRIVATE AIRFIELD outside Taos, where he would be helicoptered to Edward J. Robinson III's current home—one of those huge chalet-style mansions tucked away on the mountainside. Peter had read online about its incredible heli-skiing in Taos. But no helicopter was waiting for him. Instead, a driver stood at the ramshackle building used as a terminal. This place was not luxurious, Peter noted. Not what he had expected from private aviation. Well, maybe Taos was a little more low-key.

"Heavy weather coming in," the driver explained. "Choppers are shut down. Your host keeps a Ford F-150 here at the FBO for guests. I can drive you if you'd like."

Peter made a mental note to find out what FBO stood for. He was a little disappointed about the helicopter, because that sounded like part 2 of this whole travel fantasy.

"I thought the storm wasn't coming in until around two in the morning," Peter said nervously.

"It's probably coming in sooner," the driver said, depositing Peter's bag next to the most high-end pickup Peter had ever seen. Peter, who knew his way around trucks, noticed that the tires appeared a little worn, but everything else seemed perfect.

"No, I've got this," Peter said asserting his independence. "Where are the keys?"

"Are you sure? It would be my pleasure to drive you to your destination."

"No, I'm good."

"The directions are on the front seat," the driver said. "The key fob is lodged in the visor." Ah, just like Mesquite Pete liked it. Working-class style. There is something about jumping into your beat-up truck (though this vehicle was far from beat up) that you leave unlocked, because who would bother to steal it? Drop the keys from the visor and off you go. Just like the good ol' days but with a lot more power.

"Once you get into the mountains," the driver was saying, "you can lose cell service pretty quick."

"I appreciate the heads-up," Peter said. Who needed cell service? With a good playlist and Lady Luck—his lucky satchel—in the passenger seat, he was ready to roll.

"Be safe," the driver said. "You may want to get back here a little sooner than you planned, to be sure we can get you home. Pay attention to the turn-offs. These mountain roads can get a little confusing. We wouldn't want you to get lost."

Peter nodded thoughtfully. He considered for a moment the idea of taking the driver up on his offer. If the weather was so bad that they were shutting down the helicopters, maybe driving himself into the mountains, along unfamiliar roads, wasn't that great an idea. *Nah*, he told himself. He'd figure it out. He was up for the adventure. He was going to drive himself. No way was he going to give up the opportunity to sign this deal, possibly meet a whole bunch of hedge fund dudes, and finally put his company on the map.

And besides, he really needed the deal. He took the key fob from the visor and slid it into his pocket.

Turning the motor over, to his delight, the engine was about as powerful as any engine in any vehicle he had ever driven. *I'll be fine*, he told himself as he steered out of the parking lot. He waved at the driver and started to make his way up toward Eddy's house.

As he drove, Peter rehearsed the details of the deal in his mind. First, he would be overseeing the complete remodel of the current home, Eddy's grandfather's house, a six-thousand-square-foot chalet that had been built decades earlier, when Taos was just getting started. It would ultimately become the guest house, as Eddy would be building a much larger house. The new one would be the main house, a compound with plenty of bedrooms and a boardroom so that he could host a dozen or more guests for shareholder meetings—or whatever kind of meetings hedge fund guys conducted—and then get in some of the best skiing in the world.

Since the original house and the soon-to-be-built megacompound were some distance from the slopes and the nearest lift, the billionaire new owner of the ski resort had agreed to build a private gondola for Eddy. The brash new owner had taken a liking to Eddy and convinced him to develop his grandfather's mountain ranchland into a swanky playground for the rich and famous. This future elite development might just garner Taos acclaim as the Aspen of New Mexico.

Eddy had inherited his father's massive fortune, derived chiefly from real estate and a bit of petroleum on the side. People clamored to be in Eddy's orbit. His fund was by invitation only, with minimum investments of $100 million. It certainly seemed big time, Peter thought.

Eddy said he had always dreamed of taking his grandfather's house and adjacent land and making a true destination property. He had just never been able to conceive of the right solution until Peter entered the picture. Peter's design of the new house and outbuildings was spectacular. This spurred Eddy to share his ultimate vision for a high-end residential development for all of his friends.

Peter's initial thoughts had blown Eddy away. Peter was able to create what Eddy had never been able to put into words—or pictures for that matter. Translating his thoughts to something tangible was a real gift. Convincing Eddy's wife, Trish, had been the hard part for Eddy. But after half a dozen meetings and dinners, Trish had finally, if somewhat reluctantly, given the okay, and Peter and Eddy had shaken hands on the general scope of the deal in the grill room at Eddy's club.

A light snow had begun to fall as Peter completed the sixty-minute drive from the airport to Eddy's home high in the mountains. When Peter arrived, a uniformed butler—the first butler Peter had ever seen outside of the movies—took his overcoat and motioned for the briefcase. Peter wasn't sure whether he should surrender his good luck charm or not, but then he realized that he would look like a run-of-the-mill salesman if he walked into a room full of hedge fund guys carrying a beat-up satchel case. So he handed it over. The butler took Lady Luck with the slightest bit of disdain and put her, along with Peter's coat, in the front hall closet.

Suddenly, Peter found himself swept up by Eddy, a tall, good-looking man the same age as Peter but who was as comfortable around great wealth as a man could be.

"Great to see you, Peter!"

Eddy bear-hugged him and led him into the great room of the house, where the party, to celebrate the merger of two other hedge funds into Eddy's firm, was well under way. Alcohol had made the party loud and boisterous.

"Fellas, meet Peter Christiansen," Eddy announced. "He builds great houses in Dallas. You should get to know him. He's an up-and-comer for sure."

A few people glanced at Peter, nodded, and returned to their conversations. Peter scanned the room. *If I did houses for just three or four of these guys, I'd be on the map and not just in Dallas,* Peter thought as he tried to act the part.

"What's your poison, Pete?" Eddy asked, pointing at Peter while motioning toward one of the servers. "You're a bourbon man, right?"

Peter was not a bourbon man, but he soon had a glass in his hand.

And then Eddy suddenly disappeared.

A couple of guests wandered toward Peter, making small talk, asking questions. Peter wasn't sure if it was the altitude, the champagne on the flight, or simply the experience of being surrounded by so many people, but he felt heady and almost dizzy. He pulled himself together, tried to keep up with the small talk, and sipped at the overly sweet amber liquid in his glass.

"Welcome, Peter!" one of the guests, a perfect Ken doll of a man, said. "Eddy's told us about you. Apparently you'll be a very good builder someday!"

Before Peter could respond or even ask the man's name, he was swept into a group of half a dozen hedge funders. They talked over each other and at each other and at Peter, and he couldn't tell if any of them were listening to any of the others.

"You built a little house for Dave Collins over in Lakewood, didn't you, Peter?" asked one of the men. Peter nodded, but as he opened his mouth, the man continued. "Such a quaint cottage of a place! I don't know how they squeeze into four bedrooms."

Another man—Peter finally realized the group was all men—put his arms around Peter's shoulders. He stank of whiskey and splashed some from his glass as he gestured toward the wide windows looking out over the valley. "Great view, isn't it, Peter?" He slurped from his glass. "Almost as good as that one," he said and winked as he pointed toward the gaggle of women clustered near the kitchen. The man made a lewd gesture as he spilled more whiskey on the enormous Persian rug and waggled his eyebrows.

"Have you met Trish yet?" another nameless man said, slapping Peter on the back as he approached from behind.

"Yes—" Peter started.

"She's a huge improvement over the first wife," the man continued. "Cheryl was a real bore. And so dishonest. She had the nerve to turn forty!"

The men all laughed, and Peter chuckled politely and awkwardly.

"Oh, yeah," said another of the indistinguishable revolving faces. "Trish is so much better . . . at spending Eddy's money!"

More uproarious laughter. Peter sipped his bourbon.

"Miss Amarillo over there," the man said, pointing behind his hand toward Trish, "has been flashing the green all over town, trying to make up for her defeat. Almost Miss Texas, but she lost to a girl from *Laredo*, if you can believe it."

"Oh," Peter said. "Did she—?"

"Spends money like a Powerball winner straight out of the trailer park, that one does!"

"That's what the wives call her—Trailer Trish!"

Peter laughed along with the group this time, trying his best to fit in. Maybe he could get some numbers of the potential clients by the end of the night. Most of these guys would be looking for a third home in a year or two.

Peter looked up just in time to catch Trish's eyes on him and the other men. His laughter caught in his throat. Trish turned back to her conversation, taking a sip of her drink, her smile never faltering.

The chitchat went on for more than an hour, which was about Peter's maximum limit. He was not prone to glad-handing and superfluous chatter about the news, weather, and sports. He was always more comfortable with a few really good friends, two or three people he could trust, not dozens of mere acquaintances. He really wanted to just sit down with Eddy, sign the papers, and be on his way before the storm kicked in.

Where *was* Eddy, anyway?

Suddenly, Peter, and everyone else in the room, could hear raised voices. Eddy and Trish. They were going at it, big time, over something. An embarrassed hush fell over the great room. Though not possible to make out the words, it was clear as daylight that Eddy and Trish were hardly seeing eye to eye. Finally, the couple emerged from a side room. Trish gave the guests a solemn glance and quickly thundered away.

"Peter, let's go into my study," Eddy said, slapping Peter on the back, attempting to be collegial and completely ignoring the awkwardness.

Alarm bells went off in Peter's head. Whatever had happened between Eddy and Trish, it wasn't good. Having been overlooked in school growing up had given Peter plenty of time to observe the behavior patterns of others. While in college, Peter had honed his skill of being able to read people.

Dutifully, Peter followed Eddy into an elegant study two stories high, with massive picture windows that allowed for what must have been stunning views of the mountains during daylight hours. Peter could see that the snow had picked up as it piled onto every branch of the trees he saw. As he glanced around the study, he noted that the room was perfect. Opposite the picture windows were floor-to-ceiling bookshelves circling a stunning antique desk. The place had the look and feel of a Swiss chalet, which might have been desirable when the home was first built, but felt a bit dated today. Still, Peter felt the same twinge of regret he always felt whenever he was in a beautiful home that was going to be taken to the studs for a full-scale remodel or knocked down simply to make way for something larger, to fit the today taste of the client without regard to the history of the property, but that was his forte.

Eddy, shaking his head sadly, motioned Peter to take a seat. The mansion's owner dropped himself into the chair behind the desk and poured two small glasses of bourbon from a bottle that said Taos Lightning and pushed one across to Peter.

"What's up?" Peter asked, but he could tell something was wrong.

"It's Trish," Eddy said, shaking his head, disgusted. "If she's done it once, she's done it a hundred times."

"Done what?" Peter asked, hoping against hope it wasn't what he was thinking.

"She hates Taos," Eddy said glumly. "But she loves Aspen."

It's the deal. I know it. She nixed the deal. Stop being paranoid, Peter. Stay in the game.

"The skiing is ten times better here than in Aspen, don't you think?" he asked without waiting for an answer. "Plus Aspen's all glitz and glamour. She says Taos is a second-rate town. I can't really argue that point. It is. But I love it here. I've been coming here my whole life. I have such fond memories here with my grandfather. Personally, Taos is a little bit more real. The rest of my life is full of flashy and showy. It's a nice break to be here. You know what I mean, right?"

Peter had no idea what he meant. His life was not yet as full of flashy and showy as he wanted it to be. And without this deal, it might never be.

"Uh, no. I've never been to Aspen," Peter said. He sat silently, waiting.

"Well, I mean you must know because you're from Mesquite. It's more of a second-rate . . . I mean less glitzy town than Dallas."

Now Peter knew exactly what he meant. But he feigned agreement by nodding his head just to get the deal done.

"She changed her mind," Eddy said bluntly. "She wants a house in Aspen. Not here."

"The location is no big deal," Peter said hoarsely, barely getting the words out. "I'd love to build your house in Aspen."

Eddy took a swig of bourbon, seeming a bit frustrated. "You're not getting it, old buddy. She doesn't want to use you. She wants to use a different builder."

"Why?" Peter asked. "I mean, we met a bunch of times, and I thought she liked the ideas. She seemed to like the plans. What *happened?*"

"Aw, you know women," Eddy said, shaking his head with disdain. "Changing their minds is what they do. It's their prerogative. I bet Catherine changes her mind all the time just like Trish does."

Eddy forced a chuckle that rang hollow for Peter.

How dare you bring my wife into this discussion. Don't validate breaking your commitment to me because you're being led around by an immature new wife, Peter fumed.

"Besides, you'll be fine," Eddy said, sounding lame. "You're a decent builder. You'll get plenty of other deals."

Oh, really? Peter thought, but he couldn't think of a good reply.

"I think the whole thing's ridiculous, but what Trish wants, Trish gets. You know, the first rule of marital bliss: Happy wife, happy life."

Peter wanted to crawl into a hole. But he forced himself to stay in the fight. "Eddy, man to man, what do *you* want?" Peter asked.

"Well, buddy, you already know what I want," Eddy said, looking sadly at Peter. "I want you to do this. I want this house to be a family compound, a place I can call home, have the kids up with their friends and maybe the grandkids someday."

Eddy gazed up at the ceiling, as if seeing the future right there in the study.

"Exactly! So, you're the one with the money. You are Eddy freakin' Robinson! She's just the second wife. She's Trailer Trish . . ."

Peter tried to grab the words from midair, but it was too late.

"*Excuse me! What did you just say?*" Eddy darted back, clearly shocked. "Don't answer that. I am going to forget you said that so we can preserve our friendship."

Peter knew he had stepped over a line and that all was lost or soon would be. He pleaded, "Come on, Eddy. You know what I mean. This is your dream. And who can build it better than me? Even *you* said I'm your guy. We've got it planned out. Let's do this. For you. For the kids. For the grandkids. For your grandfather."

"Peter, don't make me say it," Eddy said, appearing now as if he had just tasted something bitter.

"What?" Peter asked, curious, grateful that his faux pas appeared to have been forgotten.

"Trish says you can't do it. She wants to use Hunsacker," Eddy said, letting the word simply hang in the air, like a knife headed to the chopping block.

Peter's mouth dropped open. To lose the deal was one thing. But to lose it to Digby, his former boss? He could hardly breathe.

"I can do it! What is she talking about? She liked the plans."

"Well, it's not so much that you can't do it but that you are not good enough."

Peter was stunned. He felt as if every scene from his life came flooding back. You're not good enough. You'll never measure up, Mesquite Pete.

"Did you know this was going to happen? Why did you bring me out here?" Peter asked plaintively.

"I didn't *know* it was going to happen," Eddy said. "I just thought I'd be able to persuade her if you came all this way. It didn't work. I'm sorry. Maybe there's a project in town you can do for me in the future."

Peter closed his eyes. As he opened them, he saw the next level of his business vanish. All that was left was Eddy staring at him.

"Storm's comin' in," Peter said, ending the uncomfortable silence. "I think I'll head back to the airport."

"That's ridiculous. You can stay here overnight," Eddy offered. "It's going to be a nasty drive, and there's no guarantee that the jet'll be able to take off. The storm came in a lot earlier than everybody thought."

Peter shook his head. "I'll take my chances," he said, letting the bitterness in his voice ooze out a bit. "I'm not staying here, Eddy. I am going to be the best home builder the world has ever seen. I'll make a bigger impact than ten Hunsackers put together. I'll do it. You'll see."

"No, you won't," a shrill voice came from the hallway. "You'll never amount to anything other than a run-of-the-mill builder. Just be glad you got this far."

Behave. He could hear his mom's voice as his blood boiled.

"Mrs. Robinson, I will do it. You will see. I will prove it to everyone or die trying."

"I'm sorry this didn't work out," Eddy said. "I'm a little shocked you seem to be taking this so hard."

Easy for him to say, Peter thought. He's sitting on all the money in the world. Who does he think he is, using us all as pawns in his little game of chess, flying us around at his beck and call?

Rising out of his chair, Eddy offered, "I'll pay you for your time. What's your hourly rate?"

"Don't worry about it," Peter said, feeling completely insulted. Second-rate town. Hourly rate. Mesquite Pete just singing for his supper. "I'll see myself out."

And with that, Peter headed for the coat closet, where he had seen the butler—a butler, for goodness' sake—stow his coat. All the hedge fund guys were staring at him. He tried not to acknowledge them as he grabbed his coat and let himself out. A burst of wind from the snowstorm hit him as he trudged into the night.

3

DASHING THROUGH THE SNOW

PETER BANGED ON THE STEERING WHEEL, yelling at the top of his lungs in the truck. With the heavy snowfall, he was sure no one could see his rant, but at this point, he didn't really care. He started the car. *You shouldn't do this*, some deep part of his mind whispered. Furious, he peeled out of the driveway, and the truck fishtailed on the slippery road.

A heavier snow had begun to fall as Peter hastily made his way back toward the airport, devastated and shocked by the sudden loss of Eddy's project. He studied the snow as it hit his windshield. You couldn't really call them snowflakes. Thick, fat, wet clumps of fresh snow were hitting the windshield and, still more ominously, sticking to the twisty, switch-back-filled, two-lane road.

Peter gripped the steering wheel more out of anger than caution as he attempted to slow his anger and the truck, making his way through the grow-ing storm.

How could Eddy do this? I thought Catherine's Highland Park connection would secure the deal. Was it because he had laughed along with the crowd at Trish? He wasn't even the one who had insulted her.

The snow seemed to be coming in thicker and faster as he drove. Turning back might have been the prudent thing, but staying with Eddy—and, even worse, Trish—right now was the last thing he wanted to do.

Peter thought about calling his wife and checking in, but instinct told him to keep his eyes on the road and not to distract himself with a phone call. The truck skidded slightly on a particularly steep, banked curb, and Peter remembered that the tires on the vehicle were less than adequate given the conditions.

He reached over for his satchel. Lady Luck wasn't there. Had it slid off the seat? Then he remembered he had left it at Eddy's. His phone and wallet were in his bag. Stupid butler. Such a ridiculous display of wealth.

Taos had grown over the last twenty years, but not nearly as much as its better-known winter skiing siblings, Aspen and Park City. Taos was rugged and less easily accessible than its rivals. If you couldn't fly private, you were in for a long haul getting there from Albuquerque. Once you'd made the three-hour drive, though, the sense of wilderness and the heli-skiing could not be touched. Peter had never been to Aspen, and from what he had heard about it, he had no use for it—especially after tonight.

The snow was starting to get heavier. For all the advances in technology that the twenty-first century had brought, Peter thought as he gamely drove on, weather forecasting was still more art than science and, most of the time, more of a guessing game than anything else.

Catherine was funny about the weather, and she trusted the weatherman. If he said it was going to rain at three o'clock in the afternoon, she opened her umbrella at five minutes before three just in case. Peter loved her for that little quirk. He was more skeptical. He wasn't just going to trust some so-called expert. It turns out that they made a good pair. Fifty percent of the time, she was right, and fifty percent of the time, he was right. He loved her and just wanted to provide the best for her and the kids. Was that so much to ask? He had let them all down by not securing the Taos deal. Maybe it just wasn't in the cards to be the man he thought he could be. Maybe he had already reached his potential and just didn't know it. Every day, there seemed to be new evidence of this very real possibility.

Maybe I didn't deserve the deal to begin with, he thought. *If that's the case, then why am I even doing this? Am I really risking my life just so I don't have to look Eddy or Trish in the eye ever again?* Driving through the storm clearly wasn't the smartest decision. He eyed the clock on the dashboard. The drive had taken forty-five minutes earlier, along clear roads, but he had no idea how long it would take in the heavy storm. He plowed on.

Five minutes went by, then ten and fifteen. Now Peter could think of nothing but watching the swirling snow, mesmerizing in its beautiful way, clotting the windshield and burying the roadway with blowing gusts.

This is crazy, he thought. He picked up the directions he'd left on the seat a few hours earlier. Holding the sheet of paper over the steering wheel so he could still watch the road, he read the directions from the bottom up, trying to interpret the return trip. Yes, he'd passed a turnoff . . . Yes, a big curve . . . He must be more than halfway to the airfield. But would they even be flying in this weather? *I should have crashed at Eddy's place.*

That was the wrong word—*crash*. That was not what he wanted to think about right now. He'd probably have to spend the night at the airport; he hadn't seen any sort of hotel nearby. Too bad he wasn't driving through a blizzard after *someone else* built Eddy's compound and his friend's resort up here. There would be plenty of warm ports from the storm then.

Suddenly, the truck slipped sideways. Peter gasped and steered into the skid as he had learned as a teenager. He quickly regained control. *That was a close one*, he thought, and he glanced down the slope between the tall pines. He thought he might be able to see the airfield down in the valley; there was a clearing at least. Not far now. *This is the worst drive of my life. I can't wait to get it over with.*

At that moment, Peter felt prompted to pray. What was he going to do without that contract? The bitter cold outside matched the bitterness in his heart. He hated feeling this way. Was he even going to make it down this mountain? The thought of prayer made him feel even more helpless. And it felt disingenuous; was it fair to pray only when he needed something? *Dear God, I'm in a jam. I'm struggling to grow my business, and also, by the way, I'm on a treacherous winding road in a storm and could use a hand. Please guide me. Help me.* How pitiful and needy, he thought. And how arrogant to think he could turn God on like a faucet. *My hands are dirty, Lord. Let me just get in there, wash 'em under your grace, then turn your divine faucet off when I don't need it. See you next time.* Peter didn't like people who only turned up when they needed something, and he figured God felt the same way. He wasn't about to insult God with such a transaction.

Catherine was better at this than he was. He yearned for a more authentic relationship with God like she had. But he didn't know if that was possible, especially for a guy in the business world with as much ambition as he had. Maybe it was enough that he was a good provider and mostly tried to do the right thing. Hopefully, in the end, his good points would outweigh his negatives.

The wipers were struggling to keep the windshield clean. *I've been through worse than this*, Peter tried to convince himself, meaning more than just the storm, but he couldn't quite remember where or when. The truck hit another patch of ice and swerved toward the guardrail. Peter reacted, turning into the skid again, and put himself back on the straight and narrow. The truck was on the road, but his path felt wrong, like he was still sliding out of control. He slowed until he felt the road more solidly beneath him, but he felt himself accelerate again. The momentum of the heavy truck coupled with the need to get home was too great. Onward.

I wish I could pray, he thought. *If I ever could, this would probably be the right time.*

He could feel the incline of the road flattening out, like he was approaching the foothills. *I can do this*, he thought.

And then, suddenly, he couldn't.

A gust of wind pushed the pickup toward the guardrail, and Peter compensated. But the truck didn't change course; instead, it began to drift in a circle as if on a lazy Susan, still moving forward at speed. There was nothing Peter could do, nothing at all. He felt the vehicle make a complete 360 at forty miles per hour, crashing through a wooden embankment that could barely have stopped a bicycle, and then toppling over the side of the road—dropping toward the valley below.

Peter felt the world turn end over end, trees and mountain and snowbanks and sky all trading places through the windshield in slow motion. He felt the truck snag on what must have been power lines and heard the metallic twang of their wires and cables breaking. At some point he heard a loud bang, and his world filled with white, the airbag punching him in the face and chest and ringing in his ears. A cloud of powder—white as the snow outside—filled his eyes and nose. He heard tree branches cracking as the truck shot through them like a cannonball. And then he was thrown forward, the seat belt digging into his hips and shoulder as the F-150 came to a sudden stop. The last thing Peter saw was the white, wintry world still spinning as the truck landed upside down in a bed of spruce trees. And then everything went white.

4

PINNED DOWN

PETER COULDN'T HEAR ANYTHING but the ringing in his ears. He lay in a bed of thick snow, spruce trees swaying gently in the wind all around. The landscape was serene and beautiful—like a postcard except for the mangled wreckage of the huge truck. Its twisted metal and almost unrecognizable shape were anathema to the otherwise picture-perfect winter wonderland.

How did I get out of the truck? he thought groggily.

Peter, a voice said, *are you all right? Wake up, sweetie.*

It was Catherine's voice, gently stirring him awake. As he slowly pulled the world into focus, he realized he was not in the safety of his wife's arms. He was cold and in serious pain.

The snow was still coming down. He had never been in a blizzard before. Sure, he had seen snowfall in Dallas, and he had seen it snow on family ski trips, but nothing like this. All he could see was white.

Snow cascaded slowly down onto his face, making tiny drifts below his eyes that he blinked away. Attempting to move, he found that he couldn't. He was pinned between a rock and a massive tree. And even the slightest attempt to move brought searing pain.

I'm so stupid, he thought ruefully. *I never should have left Eddy's house. How could I forget my phone? I was driving too fast. Why? Stupidity. Anger. Frustration. Resentment.* His list of negative traits was piling up faster than the blizzard snow. *I really am a horrible person,* he decided. It wasn't the first time his emotion and anger had gotten the better of him.

I came out here to get a deal. The deal that would pay off the credit cards and all the other expenses. It was going to change everything. But, he said no. I remember now. It was humiliating. Private jet. Feeling like I had finally gotten somewhere in my life. I knew the storm was coming in. Went anyway. Didn't get the deal. Pride before the fall.

His neck hurt, and he wanted to move his hand to feel his neck, but he couldn't. He turned his head ever so slightly and was shocked to see what was left of the massive Ford F-150. *How did I get thrown from that wreckage? If I hadn't, I surely would have died. That's all fine and good, but look at me now. Pinned down without any hope.*

The pain was gradually becoming more intense, and so did his realization that this was how he was probably going to die. *All this effort,* he thought, *where has it gotten me? I'm face up in a ravine, in the middle of a snowstorm. The snow is going to bury the truck, then it's going to bury me. They'll find me— or what's left of me—in the spring.* He suddenly felt very cold.

I guess it's a miracle I didn't die in the crash, but now what? God sure does have a sense of humor. Who knows where I am? Wait, I was only minutes from the airport. Maybe someone is in earshot.

He yelled the best he could, but even he could tell that the snow was muffling every sound. His best effort could probably only be heard twenty or thirty yards away. *If a home builder falls in a forest . . . ,* he thought with grim humor.

He began to tell himself, over and over, aloud, "Every problem has a solution. Every problem has a solution."

I've never felt so helpless.

Just then, he heard someone say, *Pray.*

"What? Who's there?" Peter asked, astonished that someone had heard him yelling.

No response.

Through the quiet rustle of the branches of the spruce trees, he heard the whisper again: *Pray.*

"Is someone there?" Peter asked again. "Where are you?"

Still no response.

Pray. He heard it again.

"I'm over here," Peter shouted. "Right here! Can you see me? I'm here! Please! Help me! Save me!"

I'm losing my mind, he thought. *There's no one here but me. Maybe this is the first sign of hypothermia. I probably only have twenty to thirty minutes left.*

Reluctantly, Peter said aloud, "God, is that you? I'm in a real jam. I know I don't deserve to start a conversation with you, let alone ask you for anything, but I'm in trouble. Real trouble. I'm hurt pretty badly, but you already know that. I can't move. You probably know that too. See? I'm not so good at this. I'm lost. No one knows where I am. Please save me."

Peter could feel the pain subsiding. He didn't think it was a miracle from God; he knew it was the next stage of hypothermia. His body was becoming numb. Perhaps he had less time than he thought.

"Lord, I've got so much left to do still. If you could find it in your ultimate mercy to . . ."

His voice trailed off. He knew he didn't have much time, that the circumstances were too dire. He only had a few minutes left. This reality hit him harder than the crash.

It's just not going to happen for you, a voice in his head offered. It was his own voice, but with an exaggerated Texas drawl. He really was starting to lose it. *You're just Mesquite Pete from the other side of the tracks. You're not worthy of being saved.*

He tried to shake off that thinking, but he couldn't move his head more than a few inches. "God, think of Catherine and the kids. They need me. I'll do better," he promised.

Ha. That's a lie, the relentless voice scoffed.

Peter happened to agree with it, whoever it was. Telling lies in the middle of a prayer . . . Would you even call this a prayer? A conversation? A debate? A cross-examination?

Lying to God, how's that going to look on your resume at the pearly gates? the voice asked.

"Pearly gates?" Peter immediately thought of his grandmother, who had passed away only six months earlier. They had been so close. She would be standing at the entrance, waiting for him. She would be wondering, "Peter, what are you doing here so early?" By earth time, fifty years should separate her entry into heaven and his. But right here tonight, there he would be, starting his life in eternity half a century too soon.

You're in a ditch and you're digging yourself an even deeper hole, the unwelcome voice told him.

"Well," Peter replied, "if I *am* going to die right here in this ditch, at least my family will get the insurance money. Maybe it will do more for them than what I've been able to do to this point in my almost forty years on this planet."

And then something resolute in Peter snapped into place. *If I'm not dead yet*, he decided, *then I'm not going to die.*

"Stop it," he said, mustering his remaining strength. "This is ridiculous! God, save me! I promise to give my life to you if you save me."

Peter felt ashamed of how gross that sounded. *Am I really going to be that guy, the one in the movies who makes a deathbed deal with God?*

"God," he continued, resolutely, "I want to be better for you than that, better than a mere cliché. I give you my life, Lord, right here in this ditch. You see fit to either save me or send me on. It's your call, of course, but I just want you to know that I know you are in charge. I'm tired of the struggle. Your will be done. I give you my life."

Peter felt himself fading away as he concluded his prayer with two simple words: "Save me."

I don't know how I'm going to live, but God help me, I'm not ready to die. God help me.

With the remaining moments he had left, he closed his eyes and began to pray one last prayer, "Our Father, who art in heaven. Hallowed be thy name. Thy kingdom come; thy will be done on earth as it is in heaven. Give us this day our daily bread, and forgive us our debts as we forgive our debtors. And lead us not into temptation, but deliver us from evil . . . until Gabriel blows his horn."

The horn!

Peter opened his eyes and unclenched a fist still pinned to his side. He began to search his pocket on the outside of his pants with his fingers. Though he still couldn't move his arm, he could try and get to it. *There it is.* The key fob. Which side was the button on? It didn't matter. He was out of time. He just started pressing. On the top. On the side. On the bottom. In the middle.

Save me!

Harder. Harder. Harder. Less power, more finesse. *Behave.* Then he felt the small indentations of the buttons and held one of them down. The mangled F-150 began to scream into the sky, the high-pitched car alarm breaking the frozen silence. The rhythmic screeches of the alarm were like a metronome ticking off the remaining seconds of Peter's life. Practically dead on arrival in the frigid morgue of the forest, the truck had one last trick in her. One headlight flashed like a blinking eye, as if sending an SOS to an unknown good Samaritan. Maybe she was Ford tough after all.

SUNDAY

5

JIM AND MARY

PETER OPENED HIS EYES. The sky was still white, and wood stretched across his field of vision, but they were devoid of needles or even branches. Wooden beams. It was a room. He was in a bed.

Where am I? he wondered.

A skylight directly above him was covered in snow. A gentle fire in a stone hearth radiated warmth. Peter scanned the room, attempting to adjust to his new surroundings. The shelves directly opposite him were filled with books that looked read, unlike the books some of Peter's clients bought by the yard. A desk sat in front of the bookshelves. This must be a study or office of some sort. The modern art on the wall was a contrast to the traditional esthetic but gave the place a sense of tranquility.

The builder in Peter admired the room and its construction. Somebody had done a nice job here, he thought. The lines were perfect, and the room created the purposeful getaway he assumed the owner had hoped for or at least that the architect had intended.

On either side of the fireplace was a collection of memorabilia. On the left was an old picture of a group of soldiers in a field. Next to the photo was a small wooden shadow box with a medal and something inscribed on a brass plate below it. Just below that was a certificate or diploma of some sort. Peter couldn't quite make it out from the bed.

Above the fireplace, instead of a huge flat-screen TV, was a frame bearing words, perhaps a quote of some kind. The room was dim, and with the bright skylight above him, he had a hard time making out what it said. To the right of the fireplace was a sword hanging vertically from brass pegs, as if to be close to hand should it be needed.

Next to the sword was an odd-shaped item; he strained his eyes to identify it. As he saw the handle, he immediately recognized it as a tool his bricklayers used all the time—a trowel. *That's odd*, Peter thought. He wondered why such a run-of-the-mill tool would be so prominently placed. He continued his visual tour past the fireplace to the picture window where he saw snow coming down hard.

He heard the handle turning on the door off to his left, and he tried to turn his head. The pain was too much for him to move, so he settled back on the pillow.

"We sure are glad you made it, son, but that truck of yours is a goner."

"It's not my . . ." Peter's voice was raspy and dry as the words fumbled quietly from his lips.

"Don't try to speak if it's uncomfortable. You took quite a spill," Peter's host said. "I bet you're wondering where you are. Well, you're at our house in a valley about a hundred yards below Dead Man's Curve."

But who are you? Peter wondered.

"You're very fortunate to be alive," his host said, shaking his head slowly, clearly marveling at Peter's blessed outcome.

Tell me about it, Peter said with his eyes as he rolled them from one side to the other, attempting to join the conversation even if nonverbally.

He raised his eyebrows in a question, and his host was apparently a mind reader.

"Who am I?" he replied, smiling. "Is that what you are asking? Of course, that's a logical question. My name's Jim. My wife, Mary, is around here somewhere. We heard your car horn."

Car horn? Peter tried to remember. The last thing he could recall was saying the Lord's Prayer.

"I don't recall," Peter said hoarsely.

Jim offered a nod as if to say he understood Peter's situation.

"I don't think you honked the horn deliberately," Jim explained, his tone gentle. "When we found you, you were several yards away from your truck. You were lying in a ditch."

Peter began to remember.

"You were pinned between a boulder and a tree," Jim continued. "Yep, we found you between a rock and a hard place," Jim said with a wide smile at the apt and literal idiom, "half covered in snow."

"Don't mind Jim," a woman said casually as she entered the room. "He likes being a cutup. I just think he's a rascal. You'll get used to him, but you might not ever get used to his attempts at humor. I'm Mary. What's your name?"

"I don't think there'll be time to get used to his sense of humor," Peter said, straining to get the words out. "I've got to get home."

"Well, that's not going to happen for a while," Jim said.

Peter was confused. "But my wife has no idea where I am!" he insisted. "*Nobody* has any idea where I am!"

"I understand, but we're snowed in pretty good," Jim said. "You picked quite the night to go for a spin, son."

Mary said, "Tell us your name, and we'll get it all figured out."

Peter tried to sit up to take better control of the developing situation but could not do so.

"My name is Peter. Peter Christensen," Peter added. "I've really got to get back to Dallas. I was just supposed to be gone for the one day."

"Well, it looks like you're supposed to be right here with us," Mary said empathetically. "We're snowed in. It's probably going to take them a week to get the roads cleared down here. We're not exactly priority one in these parts."

"A *week*?" Peter asked, dismayed. "I don't have a *week*! What about my wife, my kids, my business? I've got stuff to do! Plus, I was only about five or ten minutes from the airport when the accident happened. We can't be too far away, right?"

Mary and Jim exchanged confused glances.

"The airport?" Jim asked. "We don't live anywhere near the airport!"

Peter tried to shake his head, but he couldn't even do that.

"That can't be right!" he exclaimed. "I should have been about five minutes away from the airport when I had the accident. That close to the airport, I'd have thought you would you be more of a priority for plowing."

Mary dropped her head ever so slightly and solemnly shook her head.

"Peter," she began patiently, "I have no idea where you got the notion that we live near the airport. That's clear on the other side of the mountains."

"That's impossible!" Peter said. "I followed the directions I'd taken to Eddy's house. Well, I had to read them backward. But I was careful to count the turnoffs. I wanted to make sure that I didn't overshoot the exit to the airport in case the sign was snowed over.

"Eddy's house is at the top of Punta del Norte Road," he said, as if it were the most obvious thing in the world. "I passed five major side roads and some big curves. Going up, it was forty minutes from the airport to his place, and I know I was driving ten miles an hour slower because of the snow. So the time works out too. I think I even saw the airport through the trees."

Jim shook his head. "Maybe your focus was a little off, son."

Why does he keep calling me son? I'm not his son.

"I know the mountain well," he said. "There's a turnoff near the top, where the road splits. If you take the left fork, that's the road to the airport. You went down the other side of the mountain, my friend. That's how you ended up here."

Peter tried to process the information, but it simply did not compute.

"That split is easy to miss on a good day. But during a blizzard, there's no way to see it," Mary said patiently.

"But my wife. My kids. My business," Peter exclaimed.

"Looks like they'll have to wait right along with that stuff you've got to do," Jim said. "Mary's right. Last night's storm buried us. This happens once or twice a winter. Nobody's going anywhere for a good seven days, I'd reckon. And you'll need to get back up and around the mountain to get back to the airport."

Jim's cavalier attitude wasn't helping Peter's frustration. Peter tried to lift his head again, felt a wave of pain, and fell back onto the pillow.

"That's impossible!" Peter exclaimed again, wincing from the effort of moving his neck. "You two seem really nice, but you've got to find a way to get me out of here. I can't *possibly* stay here seven days."

"Even if the roads open," Mary began, her tone diplomatic, "you're in no condition to move. You didn't break anything, which is miraculous. But you're bruised head to toe. With that contusion on your head, I'd be amazed if you could even stand up."

"Contusion?" Peter asked, confused. "That sounds awfully medical."

"I was an ER nurse for twenty-five years," she said. "I've seen plenty of people come out of car accidents in my day, but I've never seen anyone survive what you went through. I would be amazed if you could actually move much of anything for the next couple of days."

"Sounds like bed rest for you," Jim added, nodding toward his wife. "Just what the nurse ordered."

Peter panicked. "I can't stay here!" he exclaimed nervously. "Call 911! Get me to a hospital! If I'm that messed up, I shouldn't be here!"

Jim shook his head as compassionately as he could. "We really aren't kidding, Peter," Jim began. "We really will be blocked in for a week. There's no way they can get an ambulance down here with the roads closed."

"On top of that," Mary said, "we've got no phone service. The storm knocked out a bunch of phone lines, so that's how that goes."

"Don't you guys have cell phones?" Peter asked, bewildered. "Where's *my* phone? I'll make a call and get this resolved."

"No service down here," Jim explained. "No service, even on a good day. We are in remote territory."

"We lived in the city long enough," Mary added. "We had enough hustle and bustle for a lifetime. We like the quiet down here. It suits us. And you didn't have a phone on you when we found you."

Peter blinked a few times, trying to adjust to this new reality. He had survived a calamitous near-death fall. The borrowed truck was destroyed. On the positive side, he had no broken bones—at least, according to Mary, a total stranger. But his body felt so traumatized that he could barely feel his fingers and toes.

Cautiously, Peter asked, "Is there any chance I'll have permanent damage or even be paralyzed because of this?"

Mary shook her head. "I hope you don't mind, but I had to get a little personal with you," she began, giving him a friendly smile. "I did a routine check of your neck, your spine, and so on. Everything seems to be in good working order. Or I should say, everything *will* work once you rest up. But for the time being, you have some time to focus on resting and recovering.

"Look at it this way: It's quite a miracle you're alive and in as good a shape as you are. You could have frozen out there. I'll get you something to drink." Mary turned and left the room.

Peter turned back to Jim. "How did you get me here?"

"With snowshoes, a Flexible Flyer, some rope, and a stick of gum," Jim quipped. "MacGyver would be proud. I'm still sore from dragging you all this way."

Peter grimaced apologetically. "How far did you have to drag me?"

"About half a mile as the crow flies," Jim explained. "Only problem is, crows don't fly in a zigzag pattern in between spruce trees through a ton of fresh, thick snow. It's quite the story, actually."

"Tell me, please. I want to know how much I inconvenienced you so I make sure to repay you."

"Around these parts, we don't keep score," Jim said.

"Tell me, then. Do you think we have time?" Peter asked.

Jim smiled and, indicating the snow falling outside, he said to Peter, "We've got plenty of time."

6

ONCE A BOY SCOUT, ALWAYS A BOY SCOUT

"MARY AND I HAD BEEN WATCHING a holiday movie in the den when, suddenly, the entire home went dark," Jim began.

"What movie?" Peter asked.

"Oh, it was a classic. Want to take a guess?" Jim asked.

"Sure, something tells me you were watching . . . *It's a Wonderful Life*," Peter guessed.

"You got me. It was the Jimmy Stewart classic," Jim confessed, laughing. "How'd you know?"

"I didn't," Peter answered. "It was just a good guess."

Something in Peter had known exactly the movie they were watching. How *did* I know? he wondered.

"We sat in the stillness, contemplating the sudden loss of power when Mary asked if I'd heard something. I got up to look out the window. I couldn't see a thing.

"The nearest home is a mile away, and we like it that way. We aren't anti-social, but we lived in the city most of our lives, and we're happy to be where it's quiet.

"Mary says, 'I could *swear* I heard something.'

"I was just transfixed by the snow. It was falling so fast and so thick. I never get tired of seeing that. I figured the snow probably snapped a power line, so I told her I'd fire up the generator.

"'Like a tree falling,' Mary said, and I snapped back from the window. 'Or more than a tree. Like a whole forest.'"

Peter listened, fascinated. So someone *had* heard the truck crashing down the hill.

"That's when I heard the car horn. I went outside—freezing cold. But now the sound was unmistakable. A car horn. I realized there must've been an accident.

"I told Mary, and she went and got the binoculars. (We like to go birding.) We couldn't see anything, but we could hear the honking, so we just got going."

"Crazy," Peter murmured. He had realized his life hung by a thread, and the thread was Jim's ability to hear that distant car horn.

"We rigged a sled," Jim continued, "and we put on our warm clothes and snowshoes. We tried to hurry, because we didn't know what we'd find or how much time you had—whoever you were. And we prayed. The snow was so thick on the ground that, even with snowshoes, it would be a slog. It was a long way to the sound of the car horn. Once the snowfields near our home gave way to the beginning of the spruce forest, walking became much harder. Dragging that sled wasn't easy."

Peter felt guilty as he realized how much trouble he had caused his hosts.

"And then, all of a sudden," Jim continued, "the car horn stopped. We looked at each other like, *Now what?* So we just kept going. I mean, what else could we do? Turn back? We were moving on faith, I'll tell you that. Then we pushed through some underbrush to a small clearing. And that's when we saw the light flashing. It was the truck, or what was left of it. We moved toward the light as quickly as we could." Jim laughed.

"What's so funny?" Peter asked, feeling slightly annoyed at Jim's unexpected laughter.

"I figured," Jim said, still chuckling, "that if we didn't move quick enough to the light, then whoever drove the truck would be moving to the light himself, if you know what I mean!"

Peter nodded, thinking that Jim's sense of humor would definitely take some getting used to.

"The wreckage seemed like it used to be a truck," Jim continued, "but was almost unrecognizable. The front end was smashed, and it lay on its side, perched uneasily on what was left of a pair of spruce trees. I shined the flashlight inside the vehicle and saw nothing.

"And suddenly, Mary yelled, 'He's over here!'

"'Is he dead?' I yelled back, but Mary didn't respond.

"Now we were getting our snowshoes tangled up in the undergrowth where there was little to no snow. It felt like forever, but we finally got to you. You were lying on your back, looking peaceful, as the snow was beginning to cover you up. Mary felt for your neck and found a faint pulse."

"Holy cow," Peter said, shaking his head.

"We somehow got you on the sled. You're a big boy, and it wasn't an easy lift. I tied you to the sled; I know my knots—once a Boy Scout, always a Boy Scout. It took about an hour, but we finally got you out of the storm. You were bleeding some, and Mary took care of that. Otherwise, it was a pretty uneventful evening."

"I can't believe you did all that for me," Peter said, feeling a sense of awe at their kindness.

"The funny thing," Jim said, thinking back, "was that once we got you squared away at home, we went back to watching the movie. We had stopped by chance at the scene where Clarence, the guardian angel in the movie, says, 'One man's life touches so many others. When he's not there, it leaves an awfully big hole.' Man, Frank Capra got *that* right. We were thankful to be available to rescue you. At the same time, we wondered who might be missing you."

Jim raised his eyebrows to Peter with a combination of shock and gratitude. He was stunned, really. They sat in silence for several minutes. Peter gazed out the window at the slowly growing wall of white, contemplating the entire event for the first time.

"I guess I am lucky to be alive, huh?" Peter said as he continued to study the falling snow out the window to the right of the fireplace.

"Maybe so," Jim replied. "But in this house, we don't believe in luck."

Catching onto what Jim was attempting to convey, Peter said, "What I meant is that I am really fortunate."

"I would agree," said Jim. "In fact, I'd say you experienced a full-blown miracle."

"Sure, a miracle," Peter said.

"Don't forget," Jim added, "that Mary is a twenty-five-year career ER nurse. Yep, that is platinum good luck. As for me, I feel 'lucky'"—and he winked to show Peter what he thought of luck—"that the two of us were in the right place at the right time. Now the three of us are in it together." He finished with a good-hearted smile.

"When you put it that way," Peter gently jabbed back, "it does seem an unlikely rescue. Maybe it *is* a miracle. What do they say about luck? You have to be good to be lucky? I haven't been good enough to merit this amount of luck. So, you win. It's a miracle, my very first real-life miracle."

"For sure, it was a miracle. I doubt it is your first, though," Jim emphasized. "But the best thing you can do now is take it easy and don't sweat anything. Think of this as a gift from God, the gift of time that it sounds like you don't typically get in your day-to-day life."

"If it weren't for you guys," Peter said, "I could have gotten killed, and even if you hadn't showed up, if that truck had taken one more turn, I could've been crushed to death."

"Looks like you are just hitting the tip of the iceberg with those thoughts," Jim suggested gently. "Sounds like you will have plenty to think about over the coming days while we wait out the storm."

"I just . . . I don't know," Peter continued. "Okay, you say that God saved me, but isn't God the one who let that accident happen?"

"I think that is between you and God," Jim offered.

"It just doesn't make sense to me," Peter said.

"I'm not sure where you stand with God," Jim said, "but it seems as if you are wrestling with Him a bit. If someone chooses to acknowledge there is a God, that is the first step. Laid upon that truth are certain additional truths. God is all powerful. He created the entire universe. Everything is under His control. Therefore, God either causes or allows things to happen. So, you have your two questions: Did God cause this to happen, or did He allow it? If so, why?"

Peter was puzzled, and it must have shown on his face.

Jim said, "I'll leave you with that to ponder while you get some rest. Maybe try to rest your mind as well as your body. We've got plenty of time to figure out those big questions you're wrestling with, eh?"

Peter sighed and nodded. He watched Jim shut off the light and leave the room. Then he drifted quickly to sleep.

MONDAY

7

LIKE OLD FRIENDS

THE CROWD WAS SWAYING in unison to the beat of the music. Everyone seemed so joyful. He could feel the collective emotion—so overwhelmingly pure. He could barely see over the fans in front of him who had been standing since before the concert started. He craned his neck to see over them but was just not tall enough.

He started to stand on his seat but paused, expecting his mom to give him her infamous face that signaled her admonishment to *behave*. But this time, her expression was welcoming and invited eight-year-old Pete to new heights. He climbed up onto his seat and joined her at this new adult level where he could see it all—the stage, the lights, the band. The big screens broadcast all of it, including the swaying fans. He saw his mom on one side, singing to her heart's content. He could not hear her for the collective singing of the sold-out standing-room-only crowd at the Tarrant County Convention Center in Fort Worth, Texas. It was such a pedestrian site for the magnificence of the event. Shouldn't something this amazing be housed somewhere more fitting?

The lead singer belted out the famous lyric: "And I still haven't found what I'm looking for."

Instantly, Mesquite Pete snapped his eyes open only to hear the chorus again. "I still haven't found what I'm looking for." The singing was coming from the other room. He gathered himself through the cobwebs of returning to consciousness. The dream had been so real.

The door opened, and the music got louder. Jim smiled and said, "Good morning. Grace and peace to you. Happy Monday."

Peter simply stared at him.

"What's wrong? You seem lost."

Understatement of the year, Peter thought. *Lost. Trapped. Held hostage by annoyingly happy, joyful people. At least they are U2 fans.*

"Good morning, Jim," Peter offered half-heartedly.

"How'd you sleep? Well, I hope," Jim said.

"I was dreaming, thought I was at a concert," Peter said and noticed a cross on the wall. "So, you guys are Christians."

"Yup, we're Christians, all right." Jim smiled.

Could you smile a little less? Peter thought, but he was far too polite to vocalize the thought.

"It's okay, so am I," Peter replied. "Sort of. I mean, I go to church. I believe. Sort of."

"That sounds a little ambivalent, don't you think?" Jim asked with a gentle grin. "How's that working for you?"

"Well, to be honest, not so great," Peter admitted. "I go to church because my wife wants me to go, and it's good for the kids to see the family go together. My mom and dad were religious. But I don't really know what I think about any of that stuff."

"*Stuff*?" Jim replied, clearly tickled. "I've never really thought about the God of the universe as 'stuff.' Are you a prayerful man, Peter?"

Peter held Jim's gaze for a second and then glanced away, hoping the question was rhetorical, given how early it was in the morning.

"To be a good Christian, you have to pray, right?" Peter asked.

Jim spoke gently. "I'm not sure what you mean by 'good Christian,'" he began, "but here's a question, Peter. When was the last time you prayed?"

Peter thought about it. "I'm not sure. I'm not exactly the praying kind. Wait . . . after the truck crashed," he said happily, as if he had offered the right answer just before the buzzer. "I prayed when I thought I was dying. I didn't want to die. I lobbed a Hail Mary. Oh, sorry, no disrespect to Mary." *Behave.*

"And what about before that?" Jim probed.

Peter shrugged, or at least he tried to, but his range of motion was still nonexistent, so he lay there, thinking. "I can't remember the last time," he said. "I'm not going to say never, but I really can't remember."

"That doesn't make you a bad person!" Jim exclaimed, grinning. "You know the old saying: God loves to hear from strangers!"

"Our patient's barely awake and you're trying to sell him religion?" Mary teased Jim as she bounced into the room with a tray of something that smelled delicious.

"I really didn't expect I'd be lying here having a conversation about God," Peter admitted.

"We could talk about the Dallas Cowboys if you'd prefer," Mary said. "We're both big fans."

"Now there's a team without a prayer!" Jim said, and they all laughed.

"Seriously," Peter said. "You guys are real believers?"

"When you say 'real,' what precisely are you implying?" Jim said as Mary shot him a quick glance as if to say lighten up on the interrogation, Mr. Detective.

"You know what I mean—like, real believers."

Jim and Mary nodded as if to say *Is there any other kind?*

Peter thought for a moment. "I guess I'd like to be," he said. "But I just see all the stuff that has happened in my life growing up. Some of it wasn't so great. You know, I wonder where God was when this or that happened. Is He really involved in my life?"

"It's a fair question," Mary said. "Why don't you tell us a little bit about yourself if you are up to it. It would be nice to get to know you, since we'll be living together for the foreseeable future."

"Honestly, there's not that much to tell," Peter started. "I grew up in Mesquite, Texas. I now live in Dallas—Highland Park to be exact. My wife and I have three kids. I build houses for a living."

"Whoa, just the facts, ma'am," Mary gently chided. "That's as good a succinct, military response as I would have expected from someone else in this house," Mary said, indicating Jim. "I already feel like I have known you for years." She offered a loving smile and raised eyebrows that politely asked for more information.

"I'm just an average, run-of-the-mill guy trying to make his way in the world. I come from humble beginnings, and I'm doing all I can do to pull myself up by my bootstraps. Working hard. Trying to make it happen."

"What exactly are you trying to make happen?" Mary asked.

"My construction company," Peter responded. "I build single-family residential houses."

"Oh, that's great. Do you like doing it?" Mary asked.

"I used to," Peter admitted, a little more honestly than he had intended.

"Hmmm, what does that mean?" Mary probed.

"Well, lately, it has been more of a struggle than a joy."

"Why?"

"I'm in a very competitive market, and I keep losing potential projects that I think are in the bag. Obviously, they aren't in the bag, but I think my company is perfect for them. My team and I would do an amazing job with them. I don't know what I am doing wrong. I feel like I've lost my mojo."

"Uh-oh! Where did you put it?" Mary said quickly.

"Put it?" Peter asked, confused. "Put what?"

"Your mojo," Mary responded. "You just said you lost it. Maybe we can find it. Where did you last see it? When was the last time you remember having it? At home? In your pocket? In your car? Oh, I bet it is in the mangled truck."

"Ha, ha, ha. Very funny," Peter said, catching on.

"Actually, she's a tad on the serious side," Jim offered, "but she delivers it in such a winsome way." He glanced lovingly at his wife. "I don't mean to pry, but since we are cooped up here for the next few days, can we just pretend we've been friends for a long time? Can we cut through the niceties and be honest?"

"Sure. By the way, I've been meaning to tell you that your dad jokes aren't funny," Peter jabbed honestly.

"Touché. I walked right into that one," Jim acknowledged.

"But, yeah," Peter said, "most of my conversations on a day-to-day basis go no further than the news, weather, and sports. An in-depth conversation would be welcome."

Jim nodded. "I firmly believe," he began, "that everyone I meet is providential. It is a meeting ordained by God. Our conversation yesterday about miracles really impacted me. You, Mesquite Pete, are a miracle."

Peter flinched at the moniker. "How—"

"By all accounts, you should be dead," Jim continued. "Yet here you are alive and well—or alive and soon to be well. We were strangers before yesterday. In the same way that it was not luck that brought you here, I do not believe your previous success can be attributed to mojo."

"You sound just like Catherine, my wife. She said the same thing about six months ago," Peter said.

"Smart woman," Mary replied.

Peter raised his gaze to the ceiling and pondered a memory that floated back to mind. The room was silent as Jim and Mary waited for him to speak.

"A couple of years ago?" Peter said, his voice rising, as if he were asking a question. "My wife told me there was this really cool guy who taught Bible study to adults. I was like, *Bible study for adults? It's just stories for kids. Certainly not for adult males.* No offense, Mary."

"None taken." Mary smiled.

"I agreed reluctantly, so I showed up," Peter said, "only to find something totally unexpected." Peter thought back to the way that Bible study class had gone, taking Mary and Jim with him.

8

BIBLE STUDY

PETER ENTERED THE MANSION in North Dallas having no idea what to expect. The house was perfect down to the smallest detail. The structure was built on an oversized lot. The woodwork was impeccable. The entry way was not grandiose but welcoming, as if it were inviting a guest to discover what was just around the corner. The furniture and accessories were the epitome of traditional. Although the architecture was not exactly Peter's taste, he could appreciate the fact that each detail was copiously curated. The perfect house appointed precisely. Who was this guy who was touted as the most engaging Bible study teacher in town? Could he be any good, let alone a real Christian with all this flagrant wealth?

Peter was pleased to see a few people he knew in the big crowd. After pleasantries, everyone started filing in to the main living space, which was huge, like most of the mansions in that neighborhood. The space was perfect for entertaining—and, apparently, for Bible studies. Everyone found a seat just as the leader strode into the room at full pace.

"Good morning, guys," he said. "I'm Derek Martland, and I'm so glad you decided to come today."

His thick New York accent distracted Peter. And Derek, the Bible study guy, was a sight. He was about five feet ten inches and noticeably fit under the extra tight T-shirt. He wore skinny jeans and boots, but his boots were not Texas-style boots. They were fancy boots, with sharp tips, the kind that only Neiman Marcus might sell. The visual package was not what Peter was expecting. *Does this guy even go to our church?* Peter wondered. *I bet he goes to the happy, clappy church down the street—the nondenominational Bible church where they wear jeans or even shorts to worship.*

Peter caught himself judging Derek and immediately felt guilty. *Who do you think you are, Mesquite Pete? What do you have against Mr. New York? So what if he looks a little different or talks a little different?*

Derek cleared his throat and got to it. "Gents," he began, "let's get real. Anything worth anything takes commitment. Here's the deal. This is a one-year study. I want you to commit to showing up every Tuesday morning at six thirty a.m. for two hours. If you are not traveling for work or vacation, you are here. If you are in town, you are at chez Derek. No excuses. I've been doing this for years, and this is how it works."

Peter started thinking this guy was good—compelling. But six thirty a.m. was *early*. And every week? That was a lot. What would we talk about for two hours? The excuses flowed effortlessly.

Derek continued, "Some of you might be a bit nervous about the commitment, but my goal is to help you grow in your personal relationship with Jesus Christ. He desires a relationship with you, and part of my role is to help you get in touch with that scared little eight-year-old boy inside of you.

"We are men and yet we are running around timid and afraid. You can unlock within you, here on earth, the power that raised Jesus from the dead. You have authority to use that power to fulfill God's will for your life to glorify Him."

The crowd was completely silent, barely breathing, contemplating this extraordinary champion for Christ. Peter was drawn in by his passion. Maybe Derek *was* a real believer. And he was so on fire about the whole thing.

Derek went on about his journey with Christ and the previous groups he had led. Peter was stunned. He thought, *This guy's gonna push me way outside my comfort zone. He's gonna take me somewhere I don't want to go.*

Just then, Derek asked, "Does anyone have any questions?"

Peter's hand shot up reflexively. Oh, how he wished it hadn't.

Derek nodded in his direction.

Peter said, "Yes, I have a . . . hesitation."

Derek looked at him, puzzled. "Hesitation? I asked if anyone had any questions."

"Well, my question is this," Peter continued, sorry that he'd put his hand up in the first place. "The commitment you are asking is pretty significant, especially in the first meeting. I don't even know anything about the people in this group. I don't know what they do or even their wives' names. You want me to commit to a weekly two-hour meeting with a bunch of strangers? You're pushing me a little too hard too fast."

The guy next to Peter blurted out, "He's right. I'm in the same boat. What's the hard sell for?"

Derek smiled and scanned the room to see if anyone else was going to offer anything. Then, he politely said to Peter, "Was there a question in there somewhere?"

Peter just shrugged his shoulders as if to say, *Maybe?*

Derek nodded. "Men," he continued, "I understand what I am asking is significant and perhaps out of the ordinary for what you are accustomed to. But what you are used to does not seem to be working in the way you want it to. Otherwise you wouldn't have come this morning.

"Each of you has your own story. Each of you is here for a specific reason. My job is to be a good steward both of your time and of the calling He has given me. Life's too short to get it wrong. I am here to help you get it right. I look forward to getting to know those of you who make the commitment. Trust me. You won't regret it. Your life will never be the same."

Your life will never be the same. Peter recalled those words many times over the course of the next week. He went back and forth on whether he should take the bait. There were many convenient reasons he could gracefully bow out—early morning family commitments with little kids, work meetings, tens of other good excuses. But, at the end of the day, even a good excuse is still just an excuse. He did not typically shrink from challenges and was curious why this one in particular had him so indecisive.

Peter drove up to Derek's mansion the following Tuesday morning for the first official Bible study. He sat in the car for a moment, anxious. He was tempted to drive away. But he'd made the commitment and he was a man of his word, so he stepped out of the car.

As he approached the door, he noticed a sign over it that read God's House. It was so large that Peter couldn't believe he hadn't seen it the week before. Apparently, this man was the real deal. He was telling the whole world that he was a Christian.

As he stepped into the house, Peter felt a sense of peace about his decision. That peace continued to wash over him as he greeted his new Bible study friends. Peter searched for the guy who had been sitting next to him the previous week. He asked around and overheard one of the other guys say he had opted out. The commitment was too much for him.

Peter found himself a little shocked. Why wouldn't he just come? What did he have to lose? Peter got a good laugh at himself about how quickly his decision to commit became the right decision in his mind and how the judgment for the other fellow's "poor" decision flowed so freely.

Derek walked purposefully into the room as the men found their seats, like a man on a mission. They went around the room, everyone introducing themselves, and then Derek instructed them to open their Bibles. Derek was moving at lightning speed, flipping through what seemed like the entire Bible. Peter couldn't keep up. Derek's knowledge was unlike anything Peter had ever experienced. When he listened to a sermon, the pace was usually slow, and the pastor was reading from notes. Peter usually didn't even have his Bible with him during worship. This was going to be quite a different experience.

Then, Derek said, "Everyone turn to Lamentations."

What is Lamentations? Peter wondered. *Is that actually a book in the Bible?* He had never heard of that one before. How many books were actually in the Bible? Was Lamentations in the Old Testament or the New Testament?

Peter paused for only a second to see if anyone else knew. Several of the guys were flipping toward the front of the Bible. Peter thought, *Old Testament.* As inconspicuously as he could, he consulted the table of contents. Bingo. He thumbed to the chapter and verse Derek had instructed:

> *The steadfast love of the Lord never ceases;*
> *his mercies never come to an end;*
> *they are new every morning;*
> *great is your faithfulness.*
> **—Lamentations 3:22–23**

Derek went on to explain the verse as part of the lesson, but the teaching was already clear to Peter. In this previously unknown book of the Bible, in the recently discovered verse, the neophyte biblical scholar had received a revelation: God's love never ceases. His mercy does not end. It is renewed every day. God is faithful to that promise. This was a whole new twist on a book Peter had mistakenly judged as somewhere between a set of stories and a rule book full of commands of what not to do in life. *My life will never be the same,* he thought. *God is smarter than me, and He will forgive me every day, no matter what I did yesterday. Why am I so hard on myself when I make a mistake? Why am I not giving myself the same mercy the Creator does?*

9

THE STRUGGLE
IS REAL

"AND THAT'S KIND OF how the whole thing began," Peter said.

Mary and Jim were almost breathless as they listened to the account.

Peter glanced at his hosts, waiting for any type of response and dreading they might think him crazy.

"Well, amen to all that," Jim said, breaking the tension. They all laughed.

Peter felt a bit more expansive, having shared something so personal.

"I never really felt that whole thing," he said, "about, you know, taking Jesus into your life or having a relationship with God." Peter thought again of Lamentations, where God promised to provide the daily mercy Peter needed—and in the Old Testament, before Jesus even entered the scene.

Mary and Jim simply listened, and Peter realized that he wasn't really talking to them. He was just talking, processing out loud.

"It just never seemed . . . possible to me," Peter added.

"Why not?" Mary asked.

"My whole life," Peter said, "I figured that I'd just try to be a good person and hope that, when I got to the pearly gates, somehow that would be good enough to get me in."

"That's not how it works," Jim said. "Because you'll have missed out on a relationship with God in your life right now. Wouldn't you want that?"

"Well, how does *that* work?" Peter asked, hearing a trace of bitterness in his own voice. "Your pal God nearly killed me! If God's such a good guy, how did I end up going over the side of a road and nearly getting crushed to death in that truck?"

"But you didn't," Mary said.

"But I could've," Peter countered.

"Whose idea was it," Jim asked, his tone more serious now, "for you to get into that truck in the first place? How did that come about?"

Peter thought for a moment.

"The people I was visiting lent me the truck so I could get up and down from the airport."

"Understood," Jim said. "But, respectfully, that was not the question."

Mary glanced at Jim as if to say, *Take it easy.* Jim glanced back at her and nodded, as if to say, *I've got this.*

Peter was squirming on the inside, even though his injured body didn't allow his growing discomfort to show.

"Precisely whose idea was it to drive in a blizzard in that truck?" Jim asked, boring down on Peter. "Who made that choice?"

"*I* did," Peter admitted sullenly. "*I* made that choice. Okay? Are you satisfied? What's your point, anyway?"

Jim lowered his voice, as if to ease Peter's frustration. "And what made that a good idea in your estimation?" Jim asked.

"It *was* my idea. It just wasn't a good one. I didn't . . . I couldn't stay in that house one more minute."

"What was wrong with the house?" Mary asked.

"Nothing was wrong with it," Peter replied. "It's about as nice a house as you could ever ask for! It's fantastic! I was supposed to do a deal with a guy who lived there. But his wife overruled him. I felt so defeated and humiliated. I just wanted to get out of there."

Jim and Mary waited silently for him to continue.

"I knew it was a really bad night," Peter continued, thinking back. "They did say that I could stay over."

Jim and Mary continued to wait.

"Maybe if I had stayed," Peter mused, "I might have gotten a deal done with one of their buddies. They had a whole lot of hedge fund people over."

"Did you know there was a storm brewing when you came out?" Mary asked gently.

"They were talking about it on the flight over from Dallas," Peter admitted, nodding. "And then, when we landed in Taos, the driver at the airport said that the storm was coming in earlier than they thought. He even offered to drive me."

Mary gave him a knowing smile.

"I knew it was snowing," he continued. "I don't even know what I was thinking. If I'd gone back to the airport, it would've been shut down because of the storm. I don't know where I would have slept. I didn't even have my wallet and phone with me."

"We noticed," Mary said.

Peter nodded.

"When I left the house," Peter continued, "I just grabbed my coat and got out of there. I was too embarrassed to stick around after they turned me down. I really needed that deal, too."

"So, you were angry, frustrated, and embarrassed," Jim summarized. "You made a bad decision. So what?"

"So what?" Peter asked, and suddenly he poured out his pent-up feelings like a waterfall. "Are you *kidding* me? I'll tell you 'so what.' I nearly got myself killed. My wife and family have no idea where I am. I'm scaring them half to death. I'm putting the two of you out. I've really made a mess of things, and not just all that, but the business too. How could God even care about me if I've screwed things up this badly?"

"I think the Bible study was perfectly timed," Jim said.

"What do you mean?" Peter said.

Mary spoke up. "God was speaking to you through his word in the Bible in Lamentations."

"How do you mean?"

"The verse that you quoted was a revelation. It says it all. 'Peter, my love for you never ceases, no matter the bad decisions you make. I have limitless mercy for you. Every morning, I offer new grace to forgive you any offense. I will always be faithful to you. Forever.'"

They sat in silence, in part to honor the weight of the Lord's love spoken by one of His very own over another of His very own. Peter felt himself absorbing the conversation.

Jim asked, "Son, if God's love is so great that He forgives you every day, when are you going to cut yourself some slack and forgive *yourself*?"

"I knew I shouldn't have left," Peter admitted. "But I thought, what was the worst that could happen? I had no idea."

"I know," said Jim. "It's okay."

Peter thought for a moment. "I've gotten myself into a pretty bad jam. I feel like I'm broken from head to toe."

"Welcome to the club," Jim said. "It's only human to blame God for our lousy choices, especially when we don't like the earthly consequences."

Peter sighed. "Well, when you put it that way," he said.

"Jim, the guy just survived something that nobody should have to go through. Maybe we ought to stop giving him the third degree," Mary said.

Peter tried to shake his head, but he couldn't even do that. "I don't mind," he said.

"Peter, I know how you feel. You are the captain of your ship. You even told us you are pulling yourself up by your bootstraps trying to make it happen, right?" Jim asked.

Peter nodded shakily.

"That's a weighty job for anyone. It requires you to be really smart to make it happen. I felt the same burden when I was coming up through the ranks. And here is what I have found. There comes a point in every man's life—"

"And woman's, too," Mary chimed in.

"I stand corrected," Jim conceded. "There comes a point in every *person's* life where you've got to answer one question. Who is smarter—me or God? It may sound a bit silly at first blush, but for each living, breathing man who has an ego—"

"So, every man on the planet," Mary added, attempting to keep the mood light.

"Right you are, Mary," Jim continued without missing a beat. "For every man on the planet, his ego fuels his ambition and his plan, and he has to decide who is smarter, who knows best in any given situation. Life is full of decisions, and when it comes down to it, are you going to go your way or God's way?"

Jim paused for dramatic effect. Peter was tracking perfectly with his logic, but he appreciated the pause to consider it.

"Sometimes, when you choose your way, it lands you in some strangers' house in a blizzard, broken from head to toe," Jim said.

Peter half smiled. "The struggle is real," he added.

"The choice is yours," Jim said. "You get to decide who is smarter—you or God. If you determine that God is smarter, you can rely on His word. God's love is unceasing. His mercies are new every day. So, if the God of the universe in His infinite wisdom can forgive you, might you take a page out of His smarter-than-you playbook and forgive yourself?"

Peter sighed. "I guess I can't argue with that," he said.

Mary said, "Jim, give him a break, okay? He got the sermon. Now he gets the meal. I'll get the bouillon."

Jim laughed. "I'll give you a hand," he said.

Peter, lost in thought, watched them both go. *I still haven't found what I'm looking for.* The lyrics were stuck in his head, playing on repeat.

TUESDAY

10

DÉJÀ VU

PETER AWOKE IN NEAR DARK. At first, he thought the whole experience had just been a long, bad dream: not getting the deal, the blizzard, the accident, the two suspiciously friendly good Samaritans. He found himself hoping that none of these things had happened, that he was still at home in bed next to his wife Catherine, awakening from a nightmare scenario the morning he was due to fly to Taos.

No dice. He lifted his head weakly, and the dim glow of a small lamp on the corner of the desk showed the same room he had been in yesterday—the trowel and the sword on the wall by the fireplace, the frames on the mantel, the moonlit snow out the window. Frustrated, he lay back and sighed. The whole episode was real. He hadn't gotten the deal. He had gotten in the accident. And now he was stuck, immobilized, without a phone, not going anywhere and not capable of going anywhere. Could life get any worse?

He glanced around and saw a clock. Four fifty. But was it a.m. or p.m.? It got dark early in the winter in the mountains. Had he slept around the clock? Was it early morning? And if so, of what day? Just then, a sense of déjà vu came over him—the glow of the lone light in an otherwise dark room. He tried to put his finger on it, but the harder he tried to hone in on it, the faster it faded away. This room, the surroundings, the lighting were eerily familiar, but he didn't know why.

Slightly more frustrated than before, Peter turned his attention to his health. He tried to move his fingers and toes, which he hadn't been able to do the previous night, after Mary and Jim had taken him in. Gingerly, he sent a command from his brain to his fingers to move. And seemingly miraculously, his fingers obeyed.

What about his toes? He delivered the same message down the length of his body and received the same positive result.

Next, he tried to lift his limbs, but his muscles were too bruised and fatigued. At least his fingers and toes were moving. That was a good sign. And if his fingers and toes could come back, maybe the rest of him could as well. Maybe he was just experiencing shock. Who knew?

Peter was pleased with this slight progress. But his frustration with his overall situation overshadowed this advancement. Somewhat exasperated, he turned his head slightly and caught a glimpse of the frame over the fireplace. Inside was a needlepoint of a quote like you would find at your grandmother's house. He hadn't been able to read it yesterday, but in the dim light, he could now barely make it out. Maybe his eyes had been affected by the crash too. He had heard of something called *snow blindness*; maybe that's what it was. The needlepoint said:

> *"The heart of man plans his way, but God directs his steps."*
> **—Proverbs 16:9**

That is truth, Peter thought, processing again. *I had a plan to get the deal. God took it away. I had a plan to get back to Dallas, and God threw me over a cliff. This whole situation is crazy.*

He called out, "Hello? Jim, Mary, you guys up?"

Nothing. He tried again, louder. "Hello!" He tried to shout, but he couldn't muster much volume with his bruised ribs.

Fortunately, his yelling must have been loud enough; he heard footsteps padding down the hallway.

Mary opened the door and said in a teasing voice, "Rip Van Winkle! Mind if I put more light on?"

"I wish you would," Peter said, still unable to move his head much and waiting for her to come into his line of sight.

"How long did I sleep?"

Mary turned the light on and came into view.

The déjà vu washed over him again, but Peter seized the memory this time. It was his grandmother's hospital room—the bed against the wall, the lamp casting a dim pool of light around her. The similarities to that hospital room were uncanny, notwithstanding the snow outside the window.

"You didn't sleep very long—only eighteen hours," Mary said, grinning. "It's Tuesday morning. I thought you'd sleep around the clock. I bet Jim ten dollars. I guess I lost."

"Guess so," Peter replied, and despite the misery of his predicament, couldn't help but smile. There was something about Mary. "I'm sorry if I woke you. It's really early."

"Oh, don't worry. We were up already," she chirped cheerfully. "You must be starving."

The thought had not occurred to Peter that he might be hungry. But now that she mentioned it . . . "I could eat," he allowed. "I just hate putting you guys out any more than necessary."

"We didn't bring you in from the storm to have you starve to death," Mary said. "What can I make you?"

Peter thought for a moment. "Honestly, I have no idea. I can't even lift my hands to my mouth. Whatever is easy, I guess."

"I'll make you some of my famous oatmeal," Mary said. "That will be warm and good for your system as it heals."

"That'd be great." Peter again smiled at Mary.

Oatmeal? That triggered another memory about his grandmother, who made the most amazing oatmeal. Peter didn't ordinarily like oatmeal, but he loved his Mimi's version. He could never figure out what she did to make it so delicious. She had practically raised him in tandem with his parents since they were so young when they married and could use all the help they could get. He would often spend the weekends with his grandmother.

At least once, each of those weekends, Mimi would make her famous oatmeal. Just the mention of the breakfast staple took Peter back to a homier time in his life. His Mimi was not just his grandmother; she was his friend. They bonded over trips to museums, tours of local bread companies, and burgers at every fast-food chain imaginable. She taught him to swim and offered her pearls of wisdom regardless of whether they were welcome or not.

Mary nodded. "I'm on it," she said. "Any progress? With your body?"

Peter tried to nod, but his neck hurt when he did, so he stopped. "Fingers and toes are back," he said.

Mary nodded approvingly. "It's a start. I'll work on your breakfast, and I'll tell Jim that Sleeping Beauty has arisen."

Peter tried to laugh, but it hurt too much. "I'll be right here," he said sarcastically.

"No push-ups or sit-ups," Mary warned in a gently mocking tone. "Pinkie promise?"

"I'm just happy I can move my pinkie," Peter said.

Mary gave him a nice smile and headed off.

Down the hall, he could hear Mary call to Jim: "He walks in beauty, like the night of starry skies and cloudless climes."

Peter just sighed. *Crazy people*, he thought. *But nice. Very nice.*

A few moments later, Jim swung into view and sat down opposite Peter.

"We got our beauty rest?" Jim asked, grinning.

"We did," Peter allowed.

"You got your fingers and toes back, I hear," Jim said. "That's a promising sign. It points to shock, not a physical problem. I'll take shock over paralysis any day. You should continue to recover movement over time.

"We got four feet of snow in the last twenty-four hours, and I bet we're due for another couple of feet tonight. We've got eight-foot drifts around the house. We're totally socked in. You're now officially the highlight of our week."

"I hate to be a burden," Peter said.

"You call it a burden; we call it a gift," Jim said. "We had fun chatting with you yesterday. Otherwise, what else would we be doing? It's always nice when company comes calling—or crashing in, I should say in your case."

Peter gave his best supportive smile in response to Jim's dad humor. He could hear Mary in the kitchen down the hall.

"Any new thoughts on your predicament?" Jim asked.

"Yes. Do you remember when you asked me the last time I prayed?" Peter asked.

"You mean just yesterday? Well, yes. Yes, I do," Jim responded. "I meant your physical predicament. But I can't wait to hear what you are thinking about."

"Oh, sorry. My mind is pondering this prayer thing. Anyway, I remembered the last time I prayed. I mean the last time I really prayed before the accident."

"Tell me," Jim said.

"It was about a year ago, when my grandmother was sick. I hadn't thought about it since then until this morning."

Peter closed his eyes for a moment as he conjured up the memory he wanted to share with Jim.

11

MIMI

PETER WAS WALKING DOWN one of the halls of the hospital trying to find her room. His dad had called to tell him that Peter's grandmother, Mimi, had fallen and broken her hip. Peter was devastated.

He knew that, at age eighty-nine, a broken hip was often a death sentence. He was not ready to face the reality that his Mimi might not be in this world to support him, comfort him, exhort him, or guide him like she often had in their weekly breakfast chats.

His denial was powerful. It had kept him from her bedside since the fall, a shocking four days. This was an unconscionable amount of time, given the closeness of their relationship and the real danger she was in. Shame over his weakness was with him every step down the almost empty hallway. She deserved better.

As he rounded the corner, he found her room. The door was closed. He paused before going in. Then, with what little courage he could muster, he pushed the door open.

She was all the way across the room, with a single lamp casting an aura of light around her frail body in an otherwise dark room. The effect was both ominous and peaceful at the same time.

"Hi, Mimi," Peter said.

"Peter. Welcome. It's good to see you," she said weakly.

He wondered whether that last comment was a critique on his delay in coming to see her. A guilty conscience can find validation even in the most genuine of statements.

Over the next ten minutes, they exchanged pleasantries as if they were distant acquaintances who had just bumped into each other. The talk felt awkward to Peter, but his grandmother seemed perfectly content to let him come to the conversation the best he could.

As he ran out of trivialities, Peter felt a tingling sensation all over his body, which he perceived as an overwhelming inclination to pray for his grandmother. This was odd. He had never had this feeling before, but the call to action was clear. *Pray with her.*

Peter was not the pray-with-people kind of person. Heck, he was hardly even a praying kind of person. He believed his prayers were private. His own business. He did not pray out loud or even with someone else, unless it was saying grace before a meal. This was a whole new realm. He stepped forward reluctantly.

"Mimi, do you mind if I pray for you?" Peter asked.

His grandmother perked up and said, "I would like that very much."

Peter began to pray. After some time, he finally said, "Amen."

In the silence afterward, Peter felt even more awkward. He was clear on things that made him uncomfortable: hospitals, old people, sick people, praying out loud. At this moment, he could not be further outside his comfort zone. He said goodbye quickly and made a dash for the exit.

The next day, Peter's phone rang. The caller ID showed it was his aunt. He picked it up immediately, thinking she might have news about Mimi.

"Aunt Diane, is everything okay?" Peter asked, not waiting for her to start the conversation.

"Well, I don't know. You tell me," she replied. "Did you visit Mimi last night?"

Peter could feel the sweat starting to form. Her tone sounded like *Did you finally visit Mimi last night?* "I did," he choked out.

"Did you pray with her?" Aunt Diane continued.

Round two of the interrogation had Peter in a full-blown sweat. "I did," he said meekly.

"Well, what did you pray?" she asked insistently. "I need to know."

Peter was nearing a full-blown panic. She seemed so serious. *What did I do wrong?* he thought. *This is why I don't pray with people. I don't know how to do it. It gets people riled up. I don't need this.*

"Aunt Diane, what's this about?" Peter asked, trying to slow the barrage of questions.

"Well, Mimi has been telling everyone that you prayed over her and that it was amazing. It was the right prayer at the right time for her in her time of need. She can't stop talking about it. I think it really buoyed her spirits. Everyone who sees her today is commenting on it. I just want to know what you prayed so we can continue to do that for her."

Peter was stunned. He had no idea. How was it possible that Mimi was so impacted by what he had said? He couldn't even remember what he had actually said. For the life of him, he couldn't remember anything about the prayer except "amen."

"I don't remember what I prayed. I'm sorry."

"Really?" she asked, sounding doubtful. "It was just last night."

"I know. I really wish I could remember, but I don't," Peter said.

"Well, I know these are trying times. We're all under a lot of pressure. My encouragement to you is to keep it up. Whatever the Lord said through you was comforting to her. You might have the spiritual gift of prayer."

Peter got off the call and couldn't help but scoff at her last comment. *Spiritual gift of prayer? There is no way I have any spiritual gift, let alone the gift of prayer*, he decided.

A few days later, Peter's dad called to let him know that Mimi was taking a turn for the worse. She was probably not going to make it through the night, according to the hospice nurse. He encouraged Peter to come see her one last time.

An hour later, Peter stepped into her new room down the hall. His entire extended family had crowded into the cramped space. There was no place to sit and hardly any room to walk around the bed. The room was bright, a massive amount of light flooding in from the large windows close to the foot of the bed.

"Hello, everyone," Peter said as his eyes landed on his grandmother. She was not awake. Her breathing was labored. Seeing her this way was difficult for Peter and a stark contrast to her demeanor a few nights before. Peter thought, *I don't do old people. I don't do sick people. I don't do hospitals.* He pressed on by finding an open spot in the corner to stand and wait it out.

Just as he was listening to the family talk about the day's events, Peter began to get a strong tingling sensation that ran from the top of his head down to his toes.

Uh-oh, he thought. *It's happening again.*

The inclination to pray again was palpable. He could discern it more clearly this time since it had happened before. But this time, it was slightly different. He felt he needed to pray with her by himself. Well, that was not going to happen with the whole family in the room.

Compelled by a force beyond himself, he stepped forward, cleared his throat, and said, "Excuse me, but could I get a few minutes alone with Mimi?" He fully expected that this request was out of bounds and would be seen as selfish. Each of them was entitled to be there. Who was he to ask them to leave?

Surprisingly, every single person filed out of the room without hesitation, some giving him a nod as if to say, *I understand.*

This shocked Peter. Why had that been so easy? But now the hard part, praying for his grandmother.

Peter walked over and sat down on the side of the bed. Mimi's raspy breathing had intensified. It was hard for Peter to listen to it. As gingerly as he could, he reached his left hand across her body and worked it under her neck until he was cradling her head. He worked his right hand under the small of her back. She was so frail and as light as a feather. He gently lifted her up. He put his cheek to hers and began to whisper his prayer softly to her ear.

"You have had an amazing life," he began. "You have done many things you never thought possible as a young girl on the farm in Illinois with eight brothers and sisters. You struck out on your own when that was not fashionable. You have meant the world to me. You have guided me my whole life. You have always been there for me."

As Peter continued to pray, his grandmother's labored breathing slowed and then stopped. Peter began to question what was happening, but he did not stop praying. He was getting nervous because he thought she might be passing right now. He felt his mind scrambling to honor her.

"Mimi," he continued, "your job is complete. You have finished the good race. Well done, good and faithful servant. You can go in peace. I will see you again soon. Amen." Peter finished.

As he laid her back down on the bed, he was in full shock. Had she just passed away in his arms during the prayer? If so, he was in big trouble. He had robbed the rest of the family of their moment to be with her. He scanned the room for an escape route. No second door. The windows were not the kind that opened. He was trapped.

Just then, his grandmother's labored breathing returned almost as vigorously as it had been before the prayer. Not knowing he had been holding his breath, Peter let out a huge sigh of relief. But this relief was tempered by the fact that his grandmother was still experiencing the difficulty of dying. He was not going to stick around to debrief the family.

As Peter stepped into the hallway, he said, "Thank you for allowing me to do that. I really appreciate it." After a few hugs and some additional pleasantries, Peter dashed for the exit.

12

NOT GUARANTEED

PETER BLINKED A TEAR AWAY as he came back to the present moment with Jim.

"Peter, I am honored that you shared that story with me," Jim said.

Mary had rejoined them. She moved to the side of his bed with the oatmeal that had been cooling while Peter was sharing his story. Without saying a word, she gently proceeded to feed him one bite at a time. Afterward, Peter fell fast asleep. He groggily awoke several times throughout the day and into the evening, and Mary was there by his side each time.

"What time is it?" Peter asked as he finally awoke fully.

"It's late. You slept a long time. Your body needs the rest to heal."

"I hope I didn't go too deep with the grandmother story," Peter said, suddenly embarrassed.

"Like Jim said, we were honored you trusted us with such a personal story. Seems like it was quite an experience for you."

"You can say that again. I don't know why I hadn't thought about it since it happened. She died later that night, and we spent the following week consumed with family, friends, and the service."

"Why do you think you thought of it now?"

"This room sort of reminds me of her hospital room. When you offered me oatmeal, it took me back to Saturday mornings at her house. The memories just came flooding back, I guess."

"After you finished telling us the story, you seemed lost in thought. Did God bring anything to mind that caused you to reflect on the experience?" Mary asked.

"It's funny you ask. I couldn't shake how real her death was. I mean she didn't die in my arms, but for two minutes or so, I thought she had. It was the first time I had ever thought about dying in real terms."

"Death can be scary, especially for those who don't know where they are going when they die," Mary said.

"It's not so much that. I don't think death is scary so much as imminent, for all of us."

"That's what Jim always says: 'None of us gets out of this alive,'" Mary said, doing her best Jim impersonation.

Peter smiled and then he grew serious again.

"For my grandmother," he began, "she got to live an amazing eighty-nine years on this planet. That's incredible. And, on some level, I have always assumed I will get the same. I live like I have ninety years to do whatever it is that I am here to do, to fulfill my purpose on this planet. The problem with that thinking is—well, me in this bed unable to move."

"You had me, then you lost me," Mary admitted.

"The accident. Me choosing to drive in a blizzard. I ended up putting myself in harm's way. I almost died. I really thought I was going to die out there in that ditch."

"Thank the good Lord you didn't," Mary said.

"Yes, thanks to you, and Jim too. But the point I'm realizing is that I am not guaranteed ninety years on this planet. Heck, I'm not guaranteed eighty or seventy or even sixty years. I'm not guaranteed tomorrow. Now *that* scares me."

"None of us is guaranteed tomorrow," Mary gently replied. "Tell me why that's scary to you."

"If I may not have tomorrow, then what am I doing with today?"

"I have seen my share of things," Mary said. "The most tragic of all those things have been the times I have held the hand of someone on their deathbed sharing with me the regrets of their life. I can hear the echo to this day: 'I regret I didn't reach out to my daughter and tell her I love her.' 'I regret I didn't reach out to my sister and reconcile after our mom died.' 'I regret I spent my life chasing after money, status, or acclaim.' Jealousy. Anger. Pettiness. Bitterness. A lack of forgiveness. The list goes on and on."

Peter winced with every statement of regret like a fighter absorbing a series of body blows. "Please stop. It's all landing a little too close to home."

"Oh, sorry," Mary said. "At the end of the day, I have concluded that each of them was saying roughly the same thing. They believed they missed an opportunity to do something they knew deep down they were called to do."

"And time had run out," Peter added.

"Exactly," Mary agreed.

"That is tragic. I don't want that to be me."

"It doesn't have to be," Mary said.

"It sure feels like me right now. So many things left undone as I lie here half dead," Peter said.

"Or half alive," Mary offered. "What are you going to do about it?"

"When my grandmother died, I did come face-to-face with the idea that we all die. Of course, I had known that my whole life, but I had never been presented with it so personally as being with her on her actual death bed."

"Go on," Mary said.

"When I left her room that last time, I vowed to make good use of what time I had."

"What did that look like?" Mary asked.

"I started working even harder to make my mark in the business world, in the residential construction world. I pushed my team harder. I pushed everything harder. I was not going to end my life wondering what could have been."

"Sounds like you were motivated."

"Very!" Peter said.

"What happened when you pushed?" Mary asked, putting a little extra emphasis on the last word.

"Well, that's just it. Nothing. In fact, something, but it wasn't what I wanted. The harder I worked and the harder I pushed, the worse the results."

"Why do you think that happened?" Mary asked.

"Over the course of my entire career, every time I committed to something and worked really hard, it usually worked. Not every time, but most of the time."

"And this time?"

"It didn't work. Not only were we not getting ahead, but I felt I was slipping behind. I could feel others passing me by, getting ahead of me. I didn't like that. I'm a competitor; that's not acceptable."

"Peter," Mary started, shifting into his vision so she had his full attention, "didn't you tell us that you recently started losing deals you thought you were perfectly suited for?"

"Yes. Why?"

"When did that start happening?"

"I don't know."

"Try and remember."

"I guess it was at the beginning of the year or a little bit before then."

"I see. When did your grandmother pass away?"

"A year ago. Almost to the day. The anniversary of her passing was a week or so ago."

"Do you see any correlation?" Mary asked.

"I don't know. Maybe. What are you thinking?"

"It seems to me that your grandmother's death presented the reality of your own death. That created a sense of urgency to really make an impact. But, for some reason, the increased effort didn't move you closer to your goals."

"That's it," Peter said, nodding thoughtfully. "You're good!"

"I don't know about that," Mary said. "I'm just telling you what I'm hearing."

"So, what do I need to do now?" Peter asked.

"What do you think you need to do?"

"I don't know. Try harder?" Peter was grappling for the right answer.

"Well, doing the same thing, expecting a different result . . . ," Mary quipped.

"Is the definition of insanity. I know," Peter said.

"First of all," Mary continued, "we are here for good mental health, so we want to avoid things that create insanity or frustration. God is not a God of confusion. He is a God of peace. God has plans for you. Plans to prosper you and not harm you. Plans to give you hope and a future."

Mary paused with concern. "I think we might be overdoing it a bit," she said, studying him. "Maybe you should get some rest."

"No," Peter said a little too strongly. "I mean I would like to continue. I've slept enough. I think you might have something for me that will help me unlock this never-ending cycle of . . ." He paused, trying to find the right words.

"Never-ending cycle of what, Peter?" Mary prodded.

"Never-ending cycle of . . . chasing after things. It's such hard work, and the results feel meaningless."

"Without purpose? Without a bigger purpose?" Mary asked.

"Yes!" Peter declared. He sighed in resignation at the answer set squarely before him. "So, what do I do?"

"I don't know," Mary said.

"Well, that's not particularly satisfying," Peter responded.

"Like you said, I'm good, but I'm not that good," Mary chided. "What you should do, that's between you and God."

"That's not much help to me. I'm not as close to God as you and Jim. God has never told me what to do before. Why would He start now?"

"I beg to differ," Mary said. "In the story with your grandmother, He told you exactly what to do."

"He did? When?" Peter asked. "It would have been nice for Him to flash an emergency light in the direction of the escape route I needed when I thought she had died in my arms."

Mary smiled at his literal interpretation. "When you felt that tingling sensation both times in the presence of your grandmother, what did you think that was?"

"Nervousness?" Peter answered.

"You told us you felt inclined to pray and that seemed odd, since you didn't regularly pray, right?"

"Right."

"It's possible that was the Holy Spirit nudging you to pray for your grandmother. The heart of man plans his way, but God directs his steps. You made a plan to go see your grandmother on two separate occasions. Once you were there, God, through the Holy Spirit, directed your steps. He called you to do what He needed done for your grandmother."

"But that doesn't make any sense. I'm no master at prayer. Why would God call me to pray for her when there were so many other qualified people to do it?"

"We don't know. Why God calls certain people to do certain things will remain a mystery to us. Remember, He is smarter than us," Mary said.

"But that seems so illogical. It's not intuitive."

"When I am attempting to discern God's voice, I use that exact thinking. If it's a logical thought, it is probably just me. If it's counterintuitive or not exactly logical, I press in. Often, it is God directing me in a different direction than I would typically go."

"When you say it like that," Peter said, reflecting, "it makes me think about Harrison Ford in the Indiana Jones movies. Remember in one of the movies, when he was on the search for the Holy Grail and he had to cross that chasm? There was no discernible way to get across, and the enemy was hot on his trail. He sensed the solution—a counterintuitive one. He took a step off the edge of the cliff, risking certain death. Just then, the invisible bridge formed right under his outstretched foot. Is it something like that?"

"That's about right. He had to believe in something that was not his way of doing things. Let me give it to you a slightly different way. The New Testament is written in Greek. The meaning in Greek of the word *step* in the Proverbs verse is 'a pipe that delivers oil to a lamp.'"

"What? That seems crazy. On what planet does the word step mean a pipe that delivers oil to a lamp?" Peter said.

"Apparently, this planet." Mary chuckled. "It's a little 'counterintuitive.'" She made the air quotes sign. "Don't you think?"

She winked. "Here's what the Lord has revealed to me. If I am standing still and I'm holding a lamp, but there is no pipe delivering oil to that lamp, I'm standing in what, exactly?"

"Darkness," Peter replied.

Mary nodded. "Because of the darkness, I can't see where I am going. I can't rely on my own intuitive thinking. I have to rely on God's instruction to step."

"Blindly," Peter chimed in again, as if in an improv routine.

"Precisely. I have to step out in blind faith. But when I do step . . ."

Peter finished her sentence. "There is a pipe delivering oil to a lamp." Peter's energy belied his physical state.

"Yep. You guessed it. Pipe. Oil. Lamp. Flame. Light."

"Fascinating," Peter said. "I never knew that."

"It gets better. The lamp can only give off a little light. It may not illuminate the entire path. It gives off just enough light for you to be more assured in your next step."

"And the next step and the next and the next," Peter said, joining the sequence.

"His mercies are new every day. In His mercy and grace for each of us, as we trust Him by taking the first step, He equips us with the light to take the next," Mary said as Peter nodded in agreement. "Peter, that's exactly what you did. The Holy Spirit, gentleman that He is, nudged you to pray for your grandmother. By your own admission, you were *waaaaay* outside your comfort zone—blind, if you will. In faith, you took the first step.

"That created the pipe, delivered the oil, lit the lamp, created the flame, and cast the light. He illuminated your path, equipping you to take the next step. Mister I-don't-pray-out-loud-in-front-of-other-people found the words to pray a prayer that both impacted your grandmother and that others talked about the following day."

Peter sighed. "I don't even really know what to do with what you are telling me right now," he admitted. "This is a way of thinking about God and His role in my life that I have never even conceived of before. Why have I not been told this before or had it explained to me this way in all the years I have been doing my time in the pews at church?"

"I'm not sure. Maybe you weren't paying attention or just didn't have the ears to hear. But as you've said before, perhaps God either caused or allowed your current situation to get your attention."

"Well, he's got my full attention. I'm listening now," Peter said. "I feel like this changes everything."

"How so?" Mary said with a gleam in her eye.

"This makes God very real to me. If He was the one nudging me to pray, which we have established was way out of my comfort zone, and He used that to comfort her both times, then this is a potentially real thing. This means not only does God exist but He is also active in my day-to-day life. He uses us—me—to do things. I saw it firsthand. I experienced it firsthand. I'm just not sure I know how to process all of this."

"Sounds like you are on a great track," Mary said. "I like the way you're thinking. I'll leave you to continue to process our conversation. I'm excited for you to have had that experience with your grandmother and to have had the time here to reflect on it and generate some meaty thoughts about your relationship with God."

Mary left the room as Peter's mind churned. God had been calling. Was he going to take a step in His direction or keep pushing his own way, hoping for a different outcome?

WEDNESDAY

13

CLOSE TO GOD

THE NEXT MORNING, PETER AWOKE and checked outside the window. It appeared that another foot of snow had fallen overnight. Peter sighed. When would he ever get out of here, he wondered. Spring?

He wiggled his fingers and toes, just to make sure that they were still responsive, and, to his satisfaction and relief, they were. He carefully tried to pick his head up off the pillow. To his great delight, he felt that he could do so. His neck was still stiff, but at least he was able to nod his head and shake it slowly with a little less discomfort than the day before. He was even able to raise his shoulders a little, but he couldn't sit up yet. Still, that was certainly progress.

Peter thought about his knees, which had taken a beating during his football days but which had not given him much trouble in the years since. Gingerly, carefully, he tried to move them toward one another. They moved ever so slightly. Same thing with his arms: He could not lift them, but he could move them about a quarter of an inch, so even that was a victory.

"Anybody up?" he called out hopefully, and a few moments later, he heard Mary coming down the hall.

"How's the patient?" she asked cheerfully as she came in. "We could go out and have a snowball fight today if you're up for it!"

Peter gave a weary grin. "I can move my limbs a little bit," he announced, "but I don't think I'm quite ready for a snowball fight."

"You saw we got more snow last night," Mary replied, sitting opposite him and studying him with her practiced caregiver's eye. "I must say you look better. Did you sleep okay?"

"Like a baby," he said. "I woke up and cried every two hours!"

They both laughed.

"Seriously," Peter continued, "I actually did have a pretty good night's sleep. I'm so hungry I could eat a horse. Do you think I could trouble you to make some breakfast?"

"Asking for breakfast is not troubling us." Mary smiled. "Like I said yesterday, what are we supposed to do, keep you locked up and not feed you? That wouldn't be very neighborly of us, would it?"

"I saw a Stephen King movie like that," Peter recalled. "*Misery*. It was about a woman who kept her favorite author locked up until he wrote a novel or something like that. Do you remember it?"

"Rings a distant bell," Mary said as Jim strolled into the room.

"Look who's up!" Jim said, coming over and patting Peter on the shoulder. "How's the patient?"

"Getting better," Peter said. "I can move my arms and legs a tiny bit. And my head."

"That's a positive step," Jim acknowledged. "I guess you saw the new snow. You can tack on another day or so to getting out of here."

"It is what it is," Peter said. "I guess I'm just happy to be alive. I guess God's not done with me yet."

"Evidently not." Jim smiled. "Mary said you two had quite the conversation yesterday. It's exciting to hear your reflections."

"You guys really walk it out," Peter said, shaking his head slightly and then wincing at the effort it took. "I wish everybody walked their faith out the way you guys do."

Mary grinned. "So do we," she said. "If we can help other people do that, we had a good day. I'll go see about some breakfast for you. You seem like an eggs and bacon kind of guy today."

"Sounds perfect," Peter replied, and Mary headed off.

"I was just thinking about our conversations so far," Peter said. "I mean, all I can do is lie here and think."

"You'll have to forgive us," Jim said. "We are very passionate about our faith."

Peter tried to put up a hand as if to say not at all, but he could only move his fingers about an inch. "It's all good," he said. "I mean, when you think about it, what else is there to talk about?"

"We could talk about the news, weather, and sports," Jim said, smiling.

"No, what I'm saying is, it's not really a time for small talk," Peter said. "In a weird way, I've never felt this close to God."

Jim nodded. "It wasn't quite the white light experience," he said, "but I guess you were merely two seconds from shaking hands with the Big Guy."

Peter tried to nod, but moving his neck was still painful, so he stopped. "About as close as I'd like to come for the time being," he admitted. "But I guess I'm beginning to realize that God is smarter than me. The reflection on my grandmother really blew me away. I feel like things are starting to make some sense for once in a long time."

Jim nodded. "I can only imagine."

Peter thought for a moment. "So why do *you* think I survived?" he asked Jim, gazing directly at his host. "Do you think there was a reason, or was it just random? I mean, some people have accidents and get killed, and some people pull through. Why did I pull through?"

"I think the question you might be looking for is *Why did God save you?*" Jim smiled.

Peter shrugged, and to his surprise, he found that it didn't hurt. Feeling the pressure of the God-sized question hanging in the morning air, he blurted out, "Jesus."

"I beg your pardon?" Jim asked.

"Jesus. I was always told in Sunday school that if you don't know the answer, then just say 'Jesus.' Apparently Jesus is the answer to any question like that."

"Is that your final answer?" Jim said playfully.

Peter smiled back, getting Jim's humor.

"Well, that certainly is a good answer, generally speaking," Jim said. "And, as luck would have it, it's the right answer to this question too."

"Really? That's lucky. What do I win?" Peter said in his best game show host voice, mocking Jim.

"The prize is in the answer to the next question," Jim bantered. "If God saved you, then for what purpose did He save you?"

"That's where I run out of answers," Peter admitted.

"Once we accept Christ as our savior, does God teleport us directly to heaven?"

"No."

"Okay, then, why? Why doesn't He take us straight to heaven?"

"I don't know. Because He wants to have a relationship with us on earth?" he asked out of desperation.

"Ding, ding, ding," Jim shouted, pressing an imaginary buzzer on the arm of his chair as Peter laughed. "That's exactly it!" he exclaimed. "God wants to have a relationship with you! The same way an earthly father wants to have a relationship with his son. You're a dad, and you want to go play catch with your son, right? But sometimes he's too busy with schoolwork or his friends or playing with his toys. You patiently wait for an opening with him. Some of the best conversations happen when we play catch."

"I guess," Peter said. "My father really didn't have any time for me that way."

"God the Father is patient," Jim suggested. "If you want to have that relationship, if you want to play catch, He's right there. He's always available."

"I don't know," Peter said.

"What's the hesitation?" Jim asked.

"If you want to have a relationship with God . . . ," Peter began, almost embarrassed by what he was about to say. "I always figured if you really sold out for a relationship with God, He would make you do things you are not prepared to do."

"Like what?" Jim asked.

"You'd have to do something big like sell all your possessions and be a missionary to someplace in Africa. And that's just not my style. So my approach has been to keep God over there and I'll stay over here, and everything'll be okay—a healthy distance."

"Healthy? Hmm. How's that working for you?" Jim said in jest. "Do you really believe that? You're a logical guy. Do you know other believers who are, as you say, 'sold out'?"

"Sure, lots of them. My wife. Her friends. Others at church."

"Have they been called to sell their possessions? To be missionaries to Africa?" Jim asked.

"No, but . . ." Peter paused, seeing the flaw in his logic. "I guess you don't have to sell everything and be a missionary to Africa."

"Exactly," Jim affirmed. "You can have a sold-out relationship with God right where you are."

Peter quietly watched Jim.

"God first wants your heart. God has placed you right where you are for a reason. He needs you where He has planted you."

"That's something I have a little trouble with," Peter said. "What exactly would God need from me? What do I have to offer God?"

"God works through His people," Jim said. "Often, what happens to you—or to anyone—in life comes by God through others. Am I right?"

"I suppose," Peter allowed with a somewhat quizzical expression on his face.

"Has there been a time when you felt close to God like you are experiencing now?" Jim asked, his tone cautious.

Peter wanted to rub his chin, but that wasn't on the menu. He thought back. Maybe there was a time somewhere along the line that would answer Jim's question. On one level, he didn't feel comfortable being put on the spot, but on the other, there wasn't that much else to do, being laid up and all. So he searched his memory.

"What comes to mind immediately," Peter began, "is that my wife, Catherine, and some of our friends seem like they are really close to God. I always joke with them that I want to sit next to them when we are out so that if lightning strikes, I'll be protected by the person God will protect the most."

"That sounds like a pretty smart thing to do—a little fire insurance policy so to speak!"

Both men laughed.

"What makes them seem so close to God?" Jim asked.

"Take my friend Brian, for instance. He takes a mission trip each year either by himself or with his family. A few years back, after his first mission trip, he was talking with some of us. He shared that his trip to Cuba had a profound impact on him. Effectively, he met Jesus on that trip."

"What did he mean?" Jim asked.

"Well, he noticed that because of the decades-long impact of Communism on the country, the people were suffering. They were forced to be dependent on the government for all their needs."

"I've heard that's the way the regime wants it," Jim said.

"Exactly. According to Brian, no Cuban he met had the ability to decide what profession they would pursue. No one got to determine where they lived. No one got to choose whether they would even have meat for dinner. They controlled nothing in their lives apart from the government's dictates and intervention. But what struck Brian is that everyone he met who was a believer was so joyful. Overwhelmingly joyful, in fact."

"Oh, the people they shared the gospel with?" Jim asked.

"No. The people who had become believers as a result of previous mission trips prior to the one Brian was on. He commented that they were so joyful, seeing them was overwhelming to him."

"Why was it overwhelming?" Jim asked.

"Brian reflected on his own life and the life of his friends. He determined that our lives here in the United States are not filled with much joy at all as we run the rat race, hurrying from here to there. He wanted to know how people who had nothing and could not make their own decisions were a hundred percent joyful while we, in a free country, who have everything and can do anything we want, are close to zero percent joyful. I don't know how accurate any of that is, but it's compelling."

"Yes, it's profound," Jim offered.

"I know. He is really wired into God. He sees things others don't," Peter marveled.

"So what about you?" Jim asked. "When did you feel the closest to God?"

"I'd have to say it was last spring, during the annual fundraiser for a nonprofit. I'm on the board."

"Sounds interesting. What happened?" Jim asked.

"Long story," Peter said. "You got time?"

"I told you." Jim smiled. "I've got nothing but time. Go ahead."

14

IN THE GAME

PETER HAD PUT THE KIDS DOWN. His nightly routine was filled with reading several books, telling scores of stories, giving hundreds of hugs, and being barraged with thousands of kisses. He loved it, but spending that much time every night for three kids was taking its toll on him, given the never-ending amount of work he had left over from the workday.

On that particular night, he had another task, a dilemma. Several years earlier, he had joined the board of Camp Grady Spruce, the summer camp he had attended as a child. He went every summer for ten years. He liked the idea of serving on the board as a way to give back to a place that had meant so much to him as a boy. One of his duties was to participate in the annual fundraising campaign. Peter hated asking anyone for anything. He certainly was not fond of asking total strangers for money. In fact, he had made it clear to the board these past few years that he would not participate. Instead, he just wrote a check for the minimum amount the camp had assigned as his fundraising goal.

This year was different. A portion of the funds raised were going to support rebuilding the original cabins, which were fifty years old at this point. As a result, Peter seriously contemplated actually fundraising . . . from strangers.

He had spent the past few months designing the cabins with his board committee. When he was a camper lying awake each night, he had dreamed of the perfect summer camp cabin. While the models he drafted today as visuals to support the campaign did not include his youthful fantasies of cabins built over the water with waterslides off the roof, they were smart designs. He was proud of his work, and they were a significant upgrade for the thousands of campers each year who would experience what he had experienced so many years ago.

He had learned to water ski, sail a boat, ride a horse, and paddle a canoe, among other activities not readily available to him in town. He always admired his counselors. Each one was unique and different from the others. Chip was like a big brother who always talked to him like he was an adult. Curtis was adventuresome and a rule breaker who pushed Peter beyond his comfort zone. He would take them on all sorts of outings during nap time, when everyone else was stuck in their cabins. Russell taught him all about life, with stories that he was sure his mom wouldn't have wanted him to have heard at such a tender age. They were certainly not in accordance with her instruction to *behave*. He loved each of them. They set the table for young Peter to experience a sense of freedom and independence his home life and school life never seemed to provide.

Peter resigned himself to fully supporting the fundraising effort. But he stopped short of asking strangers for money, he would stick with just asking his friends and family. This seemed less awkward, a safer bet. As he sat down to write the email he would send to everyone, he couldn't quite find a way to approach the ask. So he just wrote about what camp meant to him. He took a deep breath before hitting send to the fifty or so email recipients. Peter wondered whether anyone would even respond. He didn't even let his mind contemplate how little he might raise. He was prepared to make up the difference. He hit send, and off it went. Who knew what would happen?

The next day, Peter scanned his emails, hopeful that at least one person had responded. There it was. One person had replied—but only one out of fifty. *Sounds about right*, he thought. He was disappointed even though he had braced for this possibility. As he read the email, however, he was astonished. The donor thanked him for his email and the genuine passion for the camp he had expressed in it. They also thanked him for asking for the donation.

What? Thanking me for asking? That is ludicrous, Peter thought.

He read on. The couple was offering a $10,000 gift. Clearly, this was a typo. Peter's goal had been just $5,000. He was daunted by even that goal. He immediately chided himself for thinking this fundraising thing was so hard. *One email for $10,000! I've got this in the bag*, he thought as he grew in confidence.

There was a catch. The donor's pledge was a matching gift. He would have to raise ten thousand additional dollars to gain access to this donor's pledge of $10,000. Peter's initial excitement turned to disappointment, and his confidence morphed into sheer dread. For Mesquite Pete, there was always a catch, always a string attached.

As he pondered his situation, he could feel himself searching for the exit. He seriously contemplated just letting the whole thing fade away. A polite thank you to the matching donor today could be followed by a few donations trickling in. By the time he wrote a check, he could unlock $750, maybe $1,000 of the matching donor dollars. He could easily pass it off as a slow fundraising year. He even convinced himself that the matching donor would be relieved that he would not have to write a check for the full $10,000. Who even did that? A half-hearted attempt would lay the foundation for a respectable showing, all of which could be forgotten quickly.

Peter had all but resigned himself to the plan as he drove to the office that morning. This was a particularly busy season at the company, and he really didn't have time to chase down a huge sum of money in donations to take the donor's bait. But, in the back of Peter's mind, he couldn't shake the fact that he was merely settling. His standard mode, competition, was not satisfied. If he could score a $10,000 touchdown, why wouldn't he?

Driving down Northwest Highway, Peter thought back to a recent conversation with his friend Brian, the one who had recently returned from Cuba on a missions trip. Brian had said something remarkable in attempting to explain the complete joy of the people he met.

"Peter, there is great joy in being on the field for God. You get the opportunity to score a touchdown. There are no guarantees. You may never score, but the sheer opportunity is the joyful reward," Brian had said.

This resonated with Peter on two levels: football and competition.

Brian continued, "Some people never lace up their shoes for God. They are not on the field. They're not even on the sidelines. They are stuck in the bleachers."

"But at least they are in the stadium," Peter offered in defense, knowing all too well the view from the cheap seats.

"Yes, but those bleachers get pretty uncomfortable over time."

Peter knew exactly what he meant. He had lived many years on the cold, hard bleachers as a spectator, watching games unfold.

"But the fans in the bleachers love cheering the team on. Isn't that good enough?" Peter said, fighting for the role of the onlookers.

"I'm not sure. Each person has his own path. All I know is that the joy comes from following what God is calling you to do, your purpose. In my experience, that usually means being in the game."

"But it's dangerous on the field, Brian," Peter said, a little too transparently. "You could get seriously hurt."

"That's right," Brian said.

Peter was hoping for a more encouraging response.

"Peter, when you lace up your shoes for God and get on the field, there is an enemy that doesn't want to see you succeed. That makes the opportunity to persevere on His behalf all the more rewarding and eventually joyful when you put points on the board. Oh, and by the way, it is the same enemy that fills the onlookers with fear that paralyzes them, keeping them from even contemplating sitting on the sidelines, let alone being in the game."

"Get hurt on the field or be fearful in the stands. These are my options?" Peter asked.

"Wow. That's one way to put it. Not very motivating. I might offer a different set of options," Brian said.

"Hit me with it." Peter chuckled.

"Good one," Brian said. "Pursue God's path for you or cower in the shadow of fear wondering 'what if.' What if I had accepted God's invitation?"

"Brian, I love the football analogy. But that being said, how do you know what God's path is for you?"

"You'll have to figure that one out for yourself," Brian had said.

As Peter sat at the stoplight moments before turning onto the North Dallas Tollway, he contemplated that conversation. He could feel the competitive spirit welling up in him.

A voice inside him said, *Don't let $10,000 go to waste, Peter. With a good effort you could deliver $20,000 to camp and move the entire cabin project forward by leaps and bounds.*

Peter glanced over at his empty passenger seat. Was God there? Was He sitting shotgun? Mesquite Pete felt more like the copilot, maybe even just a passenger. Either way, what did he have to lose?

"God, what do you want me to—" Before Peter could even finish his question, he had a flash of three things across his mind. They seemed audible even though he had heard nothing.

Peter, you will raise the money. You will unlock the matching donor's gift. You will give me the glory.

Peter was stunned. Where had that come from? He could feel himself pressing the gas pedal with a little more pressure. The car sped up as he contemplated what had just happened. As he passed a car or two, he could feel himself absorbing the comments.

You will raise the money. You will unlock the matching gift. You will give me the glory.

The imperatives, which would otherwise sound like commands, were offered in a tone of invitation. *I invite you to know in advance that you will raise the money. I invite you to know in advance that you will unlock the matching gift. I invite you in advance to prepare your heart to give me the glory.*

This drew Peter in further as his speed picked up. He passed several more cars and changed to the middle lane. Everyone knew Peter did not like being told what to do. He was fiercely independent. Mesquite Pete was bound and determined to show the world that he could do it and do it his way. He saw any suggestion of another way to do something as unwanted support that would taint any accomplishment. He was going to pull himself up by his bootstraps or die trying.

I really need to work on that, he thought.

But this was different, an invitation to join a team. He felt himself sliding into the left lane. He was energized. Speaking to the empty passenger seat, he said, "Okay, God. I'm not sure this is all for real, but I'm in. Let's do this. Let's raise some money. Let's build some cabins. Let's make a difference." He felt electrified like the jitters before a football game against a big rival.

A few weeks later, the electricity had waned. A few people had responded to his initial fundraising email. He had generated about $2,000, only 20% of the matching funds. While this was four times what he had ever raised before, Peter felt defeated. With only a few weeks left in the campaign, he was a million miles from his goal—an insurmountable gap, not humanly possible.

As a competitive, strategy-minded businessman, he could do the math. His response rate was too low. Many had not even responded to the first email. The average gift from those who did respond was too small. Even if those stats improved, he knew that the number of people he had originally reached out to was too small to get the job done. He would have to reach out to more people. This terrified him. But, at this point, he was a man on a mission.

Peter sent another set of emails, this time to over two hundred people. Even more daring, he began to follow up with people who had not yet responded. This could not have been more outside of Peter's comfort zone.

First, it's an imposition to email people and ask them for money. Second, who was he to follow up on that initial email? He'd have to say, "Hey, I know you didn't respond the first time. I assume it is because you are not interested. I am going to bug you by sending a follow-up. So please give to me. Please give to an organization you don't know or probably don't care about. And if you don't respond to this email, then beware: I might send you another follow-up, solidifying my status as *that guy*."

Beyond this fear, he continued. With every email, text, and phone call, Peter inched closer to his goal. He didn't receive any other large gifts, but he was achieving the goal little bit by little bit.

On the night before the end of the campaign, Peter was short only $1,000. Victory was in sight, beyond his own comprehension. Making a few last follow-up calls, he found himself only $250 away from his goal. He needed one more person to say yes, and he would have accomplished something he never would have thought imaginable.

As he scanned his list for those who had not yet responded, he saw Jeanne's name. He picked up the phone and called her.

"Jeanne, this is Peter Christensen."

"Who?" Jeanne asked.

"Peter Christensen, from church. We've met a couple of times. You know my wife, Catherine."

"Oh, yes, Catherine. You're her husband?"

"Yes, I am," Peter acknowledged, feeling the awkwardness of the fact that this was not actually his relationship but his wife's.

"Okay, what do you need?" she said as if to say, *I've got a pot of boiling water on the stove I have to go tend to.*

Peter launched into his pitch. "I sent you an email regarding a donation to Camp Grady Spruce."

"Oh, now I remember. Yes, I got it. I am not interested," she said.

Peter's heart fell as her tone pierced him. This was it. Jeanne was his worst fundraising nightmare. He was bothering her. He was being too forward to ask for money. No one cared about his pet project of fantastical cabins over the water with silly little slides.

Beyond his own instincts to just hang up the phone, Peter pressed, "Oh, you're not interested? Why not?"

As he spoke, he winced. He had heard some advice in a courtroom thriller novel that you should never ask a question to which you don't know the answer. Having broken that rule, he braced for her response.

She said, "I'm not fond of the YMCA these days."

She's smart, Peter thought. Few knew that the camp was a branch of the Dallas YMCA.

"They are making business decisions that are not in keeping with their historical values as the Young Men's Christian Association." She went on with several statements that backed up her point. They were all factual and true.

Again, Peter desperately wanted to get off the phone as fast as he could, but instead he persisted. "Jeanne, thank you for sharing that with me. While I appreciate that point of view"—he could feel himself channeling his best client service approach—"that is not what I have found in all my years of affiliation with Camp Grady Spruce."

Peter went on to tell her what the camp meant to him and how it had been instrumental in forging in him the character traits he possessed today. They went back and forth in cordial dialogue. Jeanne pushed toward edgy at a few moments, when her patience was tested, but Peter stood his ground in a polite and respectful manner. *Behave*, he reminded himself numerous times.

The donation was all but lost, but he wanted Jeanne to experience the camp he knew. The camp of his youth had been such an integral part of reinforcing those life lessons that his parents and his grandmother had so faithfully instilled in him. His words were flowing so freely. He was beyond hesitation, beyond fear of what others might think. He was fully in the flow of what was in his heart—unbridled, unfiltered, and full of energy and conviction, as if someone else had authored the words and he was merely saying them.

At the end of the conversation, Peter could feel himself getting tired. He resigned himself to the fact that Jeanne would not be the magical final donor. But he felt satisfied he had presented his case thoroughly.

"Okay," Jeanne said.

"Okay, what?" Peter asked, confused.

"Okay, I'll give. I'll make a donation," Jeanne said.

"What? I mean, great. How much would you like to give?" Peter asked.

"How much do you need?" Jeanne shot back.

This took Peter aback. What was she asking? Was she saying she'd write a check for whatever number he listed? Why hadn't he called her first? He would have easily responded *$10,000, please*! This was the moment of truth. He needed $250. The average gift was only about $150. Did he dare ask for $100 over the average gift size? She was so frustrated about giving, maybe he should downgrade the ask. $50? $75? What was the right answer?

"Two hundred fifty dollars!" he blurted out.

"What?" she asked, annoyed.

"I'm sorry," Peter said. "It's just that two hundred fifty dollars will complete my fundraising and unlock a $10,000 matching gift."

"Peter. That is incredible. Why didn't you tell me that first? I love giving when there is a match. My money goes twice as far! And the fact that you have raised almost $10,000 is amazing. I can tell you are very passionate about this cause. I'm in. Who do I write the check to?" Her tone had completely changed from the beginning of the call.

After he hung up, Peter just sat there, stunned. He had done it. As he reflected on the past four weeks, he couldn't quite believe it all. People who raised millions of dollars or who routinely asked others to help with their causes, personal or professional, might not understand the significance. But Peter understood that something monumental had just taken place, even if he couldn't yet process all of it. Something important had happened.

15

GIVE GOD
THE GLORY

"THAT'S KIND OF HOW IT WENT," Peter said, embarrassed that he had told a story that made him into some kind of hero. That wasn't how he talked about himself—ever. But it seemed right to tell Jim and Mary.

"That's a great story, Peter," Jim said. "Have you thought about that story since it happened?"

"I haven't really," Peter admitted. "Why?"

"Do you see a pattern in the stories you've been sharing with me these past few days?" Jim asked.

"How do you mean?" Peter asked.

"Well, it seems that some amazing things have happened to you, but you haven't really taken the time to reflect on them."

"What would be the point in that?" Peter asked, sounding defensive. "What happens to you just happens. You experience something and then get on down the road."

"I get that when bad things happen, we want to move past them," Jim began, "but you are asking me certain questions about God. Serious questions. Before you told me that story, I asked you if you could remember a time when you felt close to God, and you just told me this amazing story of His work in your life. It seems that God is active in your life and you are not recognizing it, either because you haven't taken the time to reflect on it or because you don't want to acknowledge it for some reason."

Peter said nothing. His face felt warm.

Jim broke the silence. "I just—"

"You don't know me," Peter cut in. "I have endured your Jesus talk as long as I could. I've been gracious, given the fact that I am totally immobile and held hostage by the two of you against my will. How dare you say I'm stupid or a coward. I'm beginning to think you were just waiting for me to fall from that cliff so you could enmesh me in this weird off-the-grid web you have going on here.

"How do I know you aren't lying to me about the cell service, the access to the roads, the whole thing? You better get me to civilization right now, or else . . ." Peter's voice trailed off.

"Or else what, Peter?" Jim replied.

Mary put her hand on Jim's shoulder, as if to help him recognize Peter's current state. Jim got up, gently honoring his wife's cue, and left the room. Mary offered the breakfast to Peter, which he waved off with his eyes and a turn of his head. She left it on the side table and followed her husband out of the room, closing the door behind her.

Peter stared out the window for what seemed like hours. The next thing he knew, he was waking up. From the way the light was coming through the windows, hours must have passed. A deep sense of remorse came over him as he relived the harshness he had showered on Jim. He could tell Jim meant well, but he didn't know Peter, and that's what had thrown Peter over the edge.

But if he was honest with himself, Peter realized, Jim might know him better than Peter knew himself. Jim's words were spot-on. Peter didn't want a relationship with God because he feared the rules and regulations prescribed by the Bible. He would be trading all of his fun and freedom for the unknown. Peter hated to admit it, but it was true. He just didn't appreciate Jim seeing him so transparently. Over the course of his whole life, he had mastered the art of building a protective wall to keep the prying eyes of someone like Jim at a distance.

Just then Peter heard a light knock on the door.

"Come in."

"Good afternoon, Peter," Jim said cautiously. "I wanted to check on you after our little chat this morning."

Peter gave him an expressionless nod of his head.

"I may have come on a little strong, and I want to offer my apologies. Will you forgive me?"

Peter didn't quite know what to say. He was expecting Jim to defend his actions or continue the interrogation. Peter was ready for that approach. He would have offered a checkmate to his opponent's move, but this conciliatory approach was foreign to Peter. Ready for round two, he found himself disarmed.

"There is nothing to apologize for," Peter responded, deflecting the deep sincerity Jim was offering him.

"Well, thank you for that, but I wanted to let you know that I am sorry. Mary often refers to my approach as 'relentless grace.'"

"Well, I could use a little more grace and little less relentlessness," Peter said, trying to ease the tension.

"It's just that I approach life with a, well, a boldness that comes from my convictions, Peter," Jim shared. "And, in our conversations, I have sensed an openness to what God has done for you to this point in your life and what He has prepared for you in the future. Perhaps my vision for your future caused me to be a bit prematurely zealous."

"What do you mean your vision for my future? What has God prepared for me? And why'd He tell you before He told me?"

Jim nodded thoughtfully. "Throughout my years," he began, "walking alongside men while in the military or as someone deployed for God to support men just like you as you wrestle with your faith, I have seen a lot. But the pattern and trends of man are consistent. The human experience is, on some level, universal. Our goal, as men, is to control our circumstances. It's as if we are hardwired to control."

"I bet Mary agrees with you on that," Peter said, again attempting to lighten the mood a bit.

"That she does," Jim said. "Speaking from personal experience, I instinctively want to make sure I am not put in any situation that makes me uncomfortable. I'm a heat-seeking missile to secure my scene, my comfort. For example, tell me why you initially did not want to raise money for your beloved camp?"

"Because I didn't want to ask strangers for money," Peter responded.

"But *why* didn't you want to ask strangers for money?" Jim pressed.

"Because I was afraid of what they would think of me," Peter confessed, much faster than he would have had he given himself time to think.

"Exactly. In that instance, you care what others think. This produces worry and fear and acts like a type of intimidation, which causes us to not take action. If you extend yourself and they think poorly of you, that is uncomfortable. How many years did you fail to raise money beyond your own personal check?"

"Five or so. I'm not exactly sure," Peter said.

"Right. Look at that. Five years of lost boldness. Lost strength. Lost courage. Lost effectiveness. Lost opportunity for you to support hundreds of campers."

"So, you are saying that God prevented the camp from getting its money because I didn't step beyond my own fear? Is that what you are implying?" Peter asked.

"In a way," Jim conceded. "What I am meaning to say is that God is going to get done for the camp and those campers what He ordains according to His will, whether you participate or not. You can't limit God by saying no to His invitation to do His work.

"Think about it this way. If God does a lot of His work through others, then perhaps He invited ten people to raise the significant funds you raised through the matching donor. In this instance, He only needed one of you to say yes. That was you. And, by all accounts, you received the blessing for your obedience to that invitation."

"Wait! That's the problem!" Peter interjected.

"*What's* the problem?" Jim asked.

"*Obedience*," Peter replied. "That word is filled with rules and regulations. Do this or else."

"Hmmm. Is that the way you see God's word in the Bible, as a rule book?" Jim asked.

"That's what it is, right?" Peter replied. "I don't remember reading anything about the Ten Suggestions or the Ten Ideas for Having a Happy Day."

"Good point. I see it slightly differently, though. In English, the word *obedience* means compliance with an order of another. I can see how that sounds like harsh rules, especially when we are talking about the concept of a loving God. However, in the Greek, the word obedience is *sh'mah*, which means 'to listen.'

"So, when I said you obeyed what God invited you to do, the translation is that you listened. It was you who chose to follow through on that invitation that you heard."

"That's fine and all, but what's the payoff for being obedient?" Peter asked.

"When you say payoff, what do you mean?" Jim replied.

"You know, the motivation? The payoff? The reward?" Peter asked. "You said something about blessing. What's the angle there?"

"Great question. I sense a measure of skepticism in your voice."

"You are picking it up precisely. My uncle was all into this televangelist when I was growing up. He would always tell me how he was going to make it rich because some preacher on TV had told him to send in money and claim the blessing for doing so. My uncle fell for it hook, line, and sinker.

"He was always pestering my mom to do the same. Thankfully, she was smarter than that. She gave to the church and not some swindler, who, by the way, ended up being indicted for fraud. So, when you say 'blessing,' it conjures up all sorts of bad memories."

"I can understand that. It's hard to reconcile what some do in the name of God while having ulterior motives. It gives us Christians a bad name. There is a quote attributed to Gandhi that says, 'I love your Jesus, but I can't stand your Christians.'"

"Ha, that's perfect," Peter said, nodding and laughing. "I totally get that. I live that almost every day back in Dallas."

"Well, we don't know if Gandhi actually said it, but it is widely used to highlight the paradox you just offered: bad behavior by people who are supposed to be followers of Christ."

"Why do people do that?" Peter asked. "It's so hypocritical."

"Well, the best way I can reconcile it is that our faith is a place for sinners. None of us is good, according to Romans—not one of us. Jesus's ministry was specifically designed to reach those who made mistakes."

"If that's the case, the whole world is available for membership," Peter quipped.

"So true. And yet it's really hard for do-gooders to hear that truth. They want their good to outweigh their bad on the final day. So recognizing that none of us is good requires them to acknowledge that they are in the slime bucket of sin with all of us 'bad folk.' We're all in it together. There is no one who is better than the other when it comes to sin.

"To make matters worse, sin is sin. There are no degrees of sin, and there is no way they can earn their way to heaven. They must be humble enough to submit to almighty God and surrender their life to Him in recognition of Jesus being their savior. Since you have acknowledged that God is smarter than you, you have freed yourself from the bondage of the scale."

"Bondage of the scale?" Peter asked.

"Whether your 'bads' outweigh your 'goods,'" Jim declared.

"Okay, I get all that, but where does the blessing come in?" Peter asked as he worked hard to digest everything Jim was saying.

"Peter, the blessing is the relationship with God," Jim said plainly. "How did you feel when you finally raised the money that unlocked the matching donation?"

"I felt incredible. It was like some sort of miracle. I had done something so far beyond my own ability that I couldn't help but share it with others."

"Oh, really? What did you do?" Jim asked.

"Well, no one had ever personally raised that much money from individual donors. The camp leaders asked me to speak at the closing event. Reluctantly, I accepted. I recounted every step of the fundraising journey. In the end, I gave God all the credit. To do anything else would have felt fraudulent."

"So you gave God the glory for working a miracle in the task of fundraising?"

"I guess you could say that."

"Do you see it?" Jim asked jubilantly.

"What?" Peter asked, bewildered. "See what?"

"Your conversation with God in your car! You said He put three things on your heart. You would raise the money. You would unlock the matching donor gift. And . . ."

"And, what?"

"And you would give God the glory," Jim said.

Peter's jaw dropped ever so slightly as he took in the full understanding. *Give God the glory.* It washed over Peter as if he were being baptized in the Jordan River that very moment.

God was right there all the time. Peter could have a conversation with Him whenever He wanted. God had earthly assignments. He was inviting Peter to join His work on earth. And in accepting those assignments, incredible things might happen. Mimi was comforted on her deathbed. Serious dollars could be raised from strangers for strangers.

Peter could feel himself being pulled beyond his comfort zone again, and he could see that Jim could sense it too. As if he were a mind reader, he said, "Don't worry. There never was any security in the comfort zone anyway."

Checkmate.

"You can die in the field in the service of God just as easily as you can die on the sofa in service of yourself. It's your choice. Be uncomfortable with no joy or be uncomfortable with abundant joy."

Peter tried to move his head as a wave of discomfort and pain shook his entire body. "Right now, it's hard for me to be comfortable with anything."

Jim nodded. "I know, but we still have some more time for you to heal physically and emotionally."

"Do you think I will?" Peter asked hesitantly. "I mean, walk again? Get out of here?"

"I have faith," Jim said with a slight smile as he left Peter alone with his thoughts.

Peter exhaled and watched him go.

THURSDAY

16

MISSING THE TURNOFF

THE NEXT MORNING, as soon as his eyes opened, Peter immediately peered through the skylight. No snow. Blue skies. Maybe his days of being lost to the entire world would be over soon. Maybe he would get out of here at some point.

Peter wanted to keep an eye on the skylight, ensuring that the skies stayed blue and that no further storms were approaching. Jim and Mary had assured him that this was the case and that the snow still had a chance to melt enough so that the roads could be cleared and so Peter could finally get home.

Aside from his pain and immobility, the pain of not being able to contact his family was becoming increasingly unbearable. He wished that he could somehow transmit a message to his wife and children to let them know that he was all right. That was the most frustrating part of this situation, he thought as he sat there each day, helpless and disconnected.

Peter had the uneasy, guilty feeling that they must have thought he had perished. Had they called Eddy? Did Eddy even have power or cell service, or had it all been knocked out by the storm—or the flying F-150? Was a search party looking for him? Were his children losing hope? What toll was this taking on Catherine? But there was nothing he could do about it.

Gingerly, he moved his arms and legs, and to his great relief, he could now sway his feet from side to side, and he could even lift his arms off the sides of the bed a few degrees. He was so happy that he exclaimed, "WHEE!" like a little kid playing with new toys on Christmas morning.

He must have said it a little more loudly than he thought, because the sound attracted the attention of his hosts, who came quickly into the room.

"What's the good news?" Mary asked excitedly.

"I'm so embarrassed you heard me!" Peter said, his face reddening. "My feet—I can turn them in any direction. They work again. And I can lift up my arms. Look!"

Peter did the equivalent of dancing a small jig as he demonstrated his newfound freedom.

"That's tremendous!" Jim exclaimed. "High five?"

"Carefully." Peter lifted his right hand off the bed, raised it as high as he could, and accepted a gentle high five from Jim.

Mary was so excited that she kissed him on the forehead. "Best news we've had all week!" she announced. "How are we going to celebrate?"

"I'm still not exactly going anywhere," Peter said. "But it's a good sign."

Mary nodded. "You're definitely headed in the right direction. Or at least that's how it seems to me."

Jim nodded. "Definitely a good sign," he added. "God is good."

"I guess," Peter said. "Although if He'd been really good, He would have let me have this accident a mere five minutes from the airport. He would've at least let me get there, don't you think?"

Jim nodded. "From what you told us," he said, "you were pretty steamed when you were coming out of that house. After you lost the deal. So you combine the bad weather and the low visibility with the fact that you were not exactly your usual cheerful self, and it stands to reason that you missed the turnoff and that's how you ended up here."

Peter shook his head in disbelief. "But that can't be, because . . ." His voice dropped off. "Well, I guess it *can* be."

Jim and Mary said nothing.

"You're right," he said. "I missed the turnoff. I can't believe it, but I missed the turnoff. I missed the deal with Eddy. I missed the growth of my company. I missed hitching my wagon to the superstar builder of Texas. I feel like I missed my whole life—or, at least, what it could have been. Missing the turnoff, it's just par for the course for ol' Mesquite Pete."

Jim nodded. "I understand how you feel," he began. "Life isn't always a steady line on a growth chart, up and to the right, no matter how much we want it to be."

"You got me there," Peter said. "I certainly took several steps back when I was leaving that house. All I was thinking about was getting out of there as fast as humanly possible. I just wanted to leave in the worst way."

"And that's exactly how you left," Jim said. "In the worst way."

"So where do we go from here?" Peter asked. "When I look back at my whole life, it's one missed turnoff after another. If God has a plan, it seems like a pretty weak one from my perspective."

"You can't blame God for your choices, pal," Jim said. "That's not how the game works."

Peter thought about it. "But I don't understand why all that has happened to me in the last few years had to happen. Or even for my whole life, for that matter. I don't want to complain, but it's not like I grew up on Easy Street."

"Life's unfair," said Jim.

"Unfair is one thing, but intentionally mean and wrong is another," Peter said.

"Sounds like you're talking about something specific," Jim nudged.

"That thing with Digby. You know . . . ," Peter began awkwardly, sorry he had even brought up his former boss's name.

"No, we don't. I don't think you've told us about him. Can you tell us?" Mary asked.

"I don't know. It's a long story and one that still stings quite a bit," Peter said reluctantly. He sighed. The last thing he wanted to do was to retell the story, but somehow, he felt he needed to.

"I got fired," he said. With his newly found muscular prowess, Peter was able to pull himself up as he began to tell Jim and Mary about the beginning of his end.

17

SUCKER PUNCHED

ANYTIME SOMEBODY TORE DOWN a Highland Park home and built a new one twice or three times the size of the original, the Hunsacker firm was quarterbacking the project. Digby Hunsacker, the founder and CEO, took an interest in the development of Peter Christensen, a young man from the other side of the tracks. He marveled at the incredible raw talent Peter possessed. He took him under his wing and taught Peter everything he knew about designing and building houses. Peter excelled beyond Digby's own expectations. His designs were genius. Clients routinely picked Peter's designs over those of associates five and ten years his senior, which left Digby both proud of his protégé and a bit envious of his talent.

As Peter continued to grow in the design aspects of the business, he established his command at overseeing the actual building of houses. Hunsacker thought that Pete from Mesquite might stumble in the client management side of the business given that he was not from the right side of the tracks. But again, Hunsacker was astonished at the skill Peter possessed. Peter had a flawless bedside manner. Little did he know that Peter's mom's constant refrain was: *Behave.* Clients who had previously said they would only work with Digby accepted Peter as their lead builder. This led to clients beginning to ask for Peter specifically. By the time Peter was thirty, he was as good as anyone in the Hunsacker crew at massaging the enormous egos of the clients who craved outsized Hunsacker houses.

Old man Hunsacker himself had three daughters, none of whom had the slightest interest in entering the family business. So Digby and Peter were a bit like father and son, with Digby serving as a surrogate dad to Peter, and Peter readily stepping into the role of the son Digby had always wanted. This suited Peter fine, given his real dad's limitations of being emotionally unavailable or just plain gone. His father had returned from Vietnam not quite right in the head. Peter loved his dad, but the man was not always able to lead the family the way Peter saw other dads doing. But Hunsacker was supportive and encouraging, and he opened up a world of professional and personal possibilities. Peter was happy to be learning, earning a good living, and supporting his family.

One Friday morning, Digby Hunsacker nonchalantly invited Peter into a conference room for an impromptu chat: "Peter, do you have a second?"

"Sure, Mr. Hunsacker. I'll be right there."

"Son, how many times do I have to tell you to call me Digby? When you call me Mr. Hunsacker, I look around to see if my dad is standing behind me. It makes me feel old, and I'd like to think we are on more familiar terms than that by now."

"You bet, *Digby*."

Peter quietly reveled in Digby's insistence on informality, feeling reassured of his place in the business and within the family.

"Peter, because we are almost like family, we can speak frankly with one another, right?"

"Absolutely," Peter affirmed.

"Well, Peter, it's come to my attention that you are bad for corporate culture," Digby said.

The words floated across the table. They seemed to be trapped in midair, a cloud of disappointment waiting to rain on Peter's head. Peter heard the words but had no ability to absorb them. He felt his jaw fall open.

After a few moments of silence, Digby asked, "Son, did you hear what I just said?"

Peter was still attempting to connect the words to his brain. He said nothing.

"Peter?" Digby repeated.

"Uh, yes, sir," Peter said, bewildered. "I'm not sure I understand."

"I said, 'You are bad for corporate culture.' It pains me to say this, because you're like a son to me in many ways. But some people think that you are not a good influence on the organization."

Peter was desperately attempting to gain his footing. He was accustomed to challenging conversations, but this one was so unexpected and truly shocking. Daily, his clients would engage him in tough topics related to their house projects. He was routinely praised for how he handled difficult situations. But this was different. This felt like something he had never felt before.

"Well, I am sorry to hear that, Mr. Hunsacker—I mean *Digby*. What should we do about this? Who are the people? Maybe I can smooth things over."

"Peter, I'm not prepared to tell you who. Frankly, it doesn't matter."

Doesn't matter? Peter thought. *The hell it doesn't.* If someone was accusing him of something, he had a right to know. He'd lost a few lucrative contracts, sure, but that was part of the game. You don't fire someone over a couple of deals gone sideways; besides, Digby had reeled the clients back in, so there was no loss to the company at all. He could feel rage swelling inside of him. He attempted to tell himself to *behave*. If he let his anger out, he knew that he might only be making Digby's case for him. This seemed so unfair. He bridled his raw emotion and channeled it to the only thing he could think of.

"Digby, how are we going to fix this?" Peter asked, his pulse racing, his teeth clenched.

"Son, I'm not sure we can," Digby responded.

He could feel his mentor—his career—slipping away. He and Digby had sat at that table many times before, working shoulder to shoulder, solving some of the hardest problems for their clients. They shared the ambition to never let a problem get them down. They were smart, creative problem solvers. Together, there wasn't much they couldn't conquer. But Peter could sense something had changed. They were no longer on the same side of the table.

Peter had never been considered a coward; he never shrank from a challenge. All his life, he had proven this to his teachers, his coaches, his professors, and now to his clients. He was a fighter. This was no different. He mustered all the confidence he could and picked up his sword to enter the fray.

"*Dig*by," he said emphasizing the first syllable of the man's name to make sure he had his attention and attempting to claw back a little of the territory that had been taken from him. "Are you asking for my resignation?"

"You know, son, I'm not sure." Digby sounded as if he had just been asked where he wanted to go to lunch. That hurt Peter even more. Firing Peter, or essentially asking Peter to fire himself, was about as difficult as deciding whether he wanted to go out for Mexican food or go to the club.

"Perhaps we sleep on it over the weekend and talk about it on Monday," Digby said, with patently false geniality. "Now, how does that sound?"

Peter was on fire inside, but he dutifully nodded his head, recognizing that his professional life hung in the balance—and Digby had his big, fat thumb on the scale.

Peter left the office, jumped in his car, and headed south on the Dallas Tollway. He called Catherine immediately. He shared the story with her. Even upon repeating it, he couldn't believe it had just happened.

"Peter, what did you do wrong?" she asked.

Indignant, Peter refrained from snapping back at her to defend himself. He couldn't. He was asking himself the same question. *What did I do wrong?*

Once Peter got home, he walked straight to his bedroom, closed the drapes, got into bed, pulled the covers over him, curled into the fetal position, and continued to question everything.

Peter and Catherine had three children, two girls and a boy, and they were living in a Hunsacker house themselves. The Hunsacker firm had designed it for a client who ran into financial trouble and couldn't afford to move in, so Digby had called in a favor at a local bank and gotten Peter the mortgage without a full down payment. But the monthly payments were huge.

The house was certainly not the biggest in Highland Park, not by any stretch, but it was not the smallest, either. Peter never liked to rely on anyone and was reluctant to take Digby's charity. But what old man Hunsacker wanted, he got. And he wanted his protégé in this house. Peter relented. *Behave!*

Up to this point, he had enjoyed living in the house. He was working hard and rationalized that he had earned it. Plus, it was good for business to live in a product of the team's effort and all. He was a team player. But now it all seemed tainted. He felt uncomfortable in his own house. He was about to lose his job because some nameless gossipers were trying to take him down. And his boss—his friend—didn't seem to give a hoot about getting rid of Peter. It didn't make sense. What kind of nightmare was this?

Sometime over the weekend, Digby informed Peter that they would continue their Friday conversation at a local coffee shop. This was a sure sign that he was going to be fired—an offsite location, a public place, far from the prying eyes of everyone at the office.

Attempting to console Peter, Catherine made a comment that was meant to be reassuring. She said, "Peter, it'll all be okay. We'll be okay."

What did she just say? "Uh, no," he said. "We won't be okay. Are you kidding me?" Peter felt himself losing control. "We have crazy expenses. We have to pay for this asinine albatross of a house. The kids have gotten accustomed to this thing called food. Don't get me started on this so-called public school; it costs an arm and a leg. Have you seen all the athletic fees, the textbook fees, the fundraising donation requests, and other fees that make it almost equal to private school? Not to mention all the tutors, private coaching, summer camps, and other ridiculous things we do to stay competitive.

But I am sure you are right: We will be okay." He never liked to fight with Catherine. But he had to put his foot down on her naïve comment.

"Are you finished?" she asked, calmly.

"No, I am not," Peter exclaimed, a little more urgently than intended.

Catherine returned the volley, "I'm just saying there is no way he is going to fire you. You're good at what you do. The clients rely on you. The company relies on you. And if he does fire you, we'll be okay."

Turning his voice down a notch and changing his tone slightly, Peter asked, "Catherine, how do you know? How do you know it will be okay?"

Catherine simply said, "I have faith."

"Faith?" Peter's voice grew louder. "Will faith pay the bills?"

"I have faith," she said again.

"What does that even mean?" Peter shot back. "I don't even know what you are talking about."

"*Peter*," she said, with a bit more authority in her voice. "It means all things will work out according to God's will."

Peter's frustration was getting the best of him, and his tone was increasingly biting.

"So, you are telling me that it is God's will that I might get fired? *Great*. Now God is against me, along with the whole world."

Catherine was calm. "I've felt this almost supernatural faith probably ever since my mom died when I was thirteen," she said as her eyes began to fill with tears.

Peter now felt like he had been sucker punched. What an idiot he was. Here he was going off on a rant, while she was doing the best she could to support him.

"If God got me through the death of my mom when I was a teenager, He can get me through anything," Catherine said tenderly. "Peter, I have faith He can get us through this. I am relying on faith that is beyond me, beyond you, beyond all of us."

She lapsed into silence, and Peter sensed she was praying for him. The thought calmed him.

He asked, as kindly as he could in his current state, "Sweetie, tell me this. If you have this gift of supernatural faith and it is so powerful and reassuring about our current situation, then why haven't we been relying on it our whole marriage?"

Catherine paused, staring into his eyes. "Peter, we have!"

A light of revelation hit Peter. He was late to the party. Catherine and God had been waiting for him to catch up for years. On that day, the Christensen marriage was solidified. A true partnership was born that would eventually lead to a new business, Christensen Custom Homes.

18

GOOD OR BAD?

"PETER, THAT IS A BEAUTIFUL STORY," Mary offered.

"It feels quite ugly to me," Peter said, still gazing up at the skylight and silently praying for continued clear skies. "I haven't gotten to the stage where I can see the beauty."

"Catherine is my kinda woman. Suffered hard times. Recognized God's hand in her life. Patiently waiting for her husband to catch up," Mary offered as she glanced at Jim and gave him a wink only a faithful wife could.

"Hands down, Catherine is the best," Peter said. "No doubt. But I don't understand what I did. Why do bad things happen to good people?"

"Whoa, big fella," Jim interrupted. "Who says you are a good person?"

"What? Are you trying to kick me when I'm down, Mr. Digby in the mountains?" Peter volleyed back, recognizing that Jim's tone was not meant to be harsh.

"The book of Romans says that none of us is good," Jim offered.

"Really? It says that? That's not very encouraging."

"Actually, it says that none of us is righteous. All of us have turned away. Basically, we are all sinners. It means none of us deserve anything. So, when you say bad things happen to good people, I want to make sure we understand what the truth is."

"Go on," Peter said curiously.

"I think the premise of the statement is faulty," Jim offered. "First off, how do you know the event was bad?"

"Because I was there. It was objectively awful. It was a betrayal. I did nothing."

"I understand that you experienced something that did not feel good. It was uncomfortable," Jim countered.

"With all due respect, it was bad," Peter emphasized.

"Peter, I know it felt bad, but do we know if this really is a bad thing?"

"Let me get this straight," Peter replied. "Are you seriously attempting to try and tell me that getting fired was a *good* thing? I mean, I like you guys a lot, and I appreciate what you have done for me this week, but I just do not think like you do."

"Peter, that's precisely what we are talking about," Mary chimed in. "God wants you to renew your mind so you can discern God's will. A key scripture helps us think through how to change our thinking and turn our mind toward Him. Second Corinthians 10:5 says, 'Take captive your thoughts, and make them obedient to Christ.'"

"I've never heard of that verse before. But I get the obedience part—rule book!" Peter poked.

"You're on to something there," Mary said. "The Greek meaning of the word *thoughts* is your spiritual capacity for truth. Take captive your spiritual capacity for truth. Your thoughts are the sponge that absorbs God's truths. Take it captive."

"Garbage in, garbage out," Jim said.

"Precisely," Mary said. "Also, the Greek meaning for the word *obedience* is a little counterintuitive. In English, it typically means to obey or abide by the rules."

"Or else," Peter offered.

"Exactly. But the Greek is different. It simply means to listen," Mary proffered. "Take captive your spiritual capacity for truth, and make it listen to Christ, the bearer of true truth. This is important because you are making assumptions and personal decisions based on feelings. Digby's conversation with you felt bad. You feel like a good person. Where is the fairness in that? Bad things happening to good people."

"Or what's even worse is if good things happen to bad people," Jim offered to further help Mary make her point.

"The reason Jim is excited for you as he hears this story is because he does not see this event as necessarily bad," Mary stated.

"Peter," Jim explained, "we don't know if the Digby conversation is good or bad. It just is. God causes or allows things to happen. And what He allows, He redeems."

Peter was hooked. The logic seemed less Christian-speak and more rational and clearer than most of what they had offered to this point.

"Keep going," Peter said.

"Perhaps God caused this to happen," Jim offered. "He can change the heart of a king in any direction He desires, according to Isaiah. What used to look like loyalty could be changed in an instant to suit the purposes of God. If He allowed Digby's actions, He certainly can redeem them for good."

"This is a little too much for me to take in. I'm not sure I even believe that God is active at this level in my life," Peter said.

"Mr. Christensen," Mary began, "resolve that issue—whether you believe God is active in your life at this level. If you decide He is not, then our conversation is over. We are not here to convince you of the hand of God. We are here to help you see the events of your life in the way God sees them. What He intended. What He intends. The stories you've told us have me believing that He has a special call on your life. He's just waiting for you."

Jim took the conversation baton from Mary, unrelenting in the pace and fervor of the dialogue. Peter couldn't help but be pulled along for the ride.

"It's possible," Jim reasoned, "that God caused Digby's act against you. You've already harvested massive fruit from Him rescuing you from the Hunsacker firm. First and foremost, He joined you and Catherine together through your awareness of her supernatural faith. Your time at Hunsacker prepared you for the launch of your own business."

"Guys, I've never thought about it this way," Peter said, feeling himself relent. "People have told me I made lemonade out of lemons, but this is an entirely different perspective. You're suggesting this was all part of God's plan?"

"What I now know, after decades of hard-fought living, is that God never demotes. He only promotes, regardless of how we feel or what we think," Jim offered. "In the long run, *bad* things are often referred to as *gifts*. It just depends on where along the timeline of your life you want to judge it. Is it good, or is it bad? I don't know. It just is. We'll let God be God and, according to His will, show us how each thing leads us to the next."

"If what you are saying is true," Peter theorized, "or at least an accurate reflection of how God works in each of our lives, then I can't really say, 'I missed the turnoff.' I can't say, 'My whole life has been one missed turnoff after another.' Logically, I have to say that all of those things were meant to be as hard as they were."

"Truer words have not been spoken all week," Mary affirmed.

"Peter, God has plans for you—plans for you to prosper. He does not plan to harm you; He plans to give you hope and a future," Jim concluded.

Peter thought for a moment, then said, "My mom used to say, 'Peter Jonathan Christiansen, I am your mother, and I have just two words for you: *Behave!*' I always thought she meant I should follow the rules, should do what I was told. Now I'm not sure that's what she meant."

Mary and Jim left the room quietly, leaving Peter deep in thought. He thought through his whole life from a completely different perspective. He could feel that this conversation would influence how he viewed his circumstances from this day forward.

FRIDAY

19

HALLELUJAH

THE NEXT MORNING, Peter awoke to the unmistakable sound of a snowblower. He blinked his eyes open and stretched so he could position himself to see the clock across the room. He was able to lift himself effortlessly off the bed. He could move the upper half of his body!

Gingerly, he slowly pulled his knees toward his waist, trying not to move too quickly, lest he somehow hurt himself further. Also, the act of movement itself was somewhat foreign, after having spent days immobilized in bed.

His legs moved. He couldn't believe it.

He wanted to call to Mary and Jim, but the snowblower outside was so loud that he figured they wouldn't hear him.

He wiggled his behind to see if it moved, and to his deep satisfaction, it did. Ever so carefully, he swung himself to a seated position. It was the first time he had been able to sit up in days—how many days, he didn't know, and it didn't matter. All that mattered was that he could sit up.

He stood, wearing the same pair of borrowed pajamas that they must have given him the day he arrived, wobbled a bit, and triumphantly walked through the door into the hall. He shuffled along the wall a bit and found a bathroom through an open door. The hallway continued for a few more feet then up some steps to a larger room—maybe the kitchen? That few feet seemed a very long distance right now.

"Unbelievable!" he shouted as he leaned against the wall.

Rising from that bed was one of the most satisfying moments of his life. But it was also exhausting. His leg muscles were not used to making this much of an effort, so he found himself almost stumbling back down the hall to the bedroom. Finding the chair where Jim had been positioning himself for their conversations, he dropped into it. He sat there for a while, grateful to be out of the bed. But the feeling crept in of how dirty and sticky he was, not having showered in days. He had a vague memory of Mary giving him a sponge bath while he was still barely conscious after the accident, but that was it.

A shower sounded delightful, but it also seemed like too much effort.

It'll come, he told himself. *No rush. One thing at a time.*

Peter wondered whether he was supposed to say a prayer of some sort right now, given the change in his condition. Formal prayer wasn't his long suit, and he wasn't sure what to say or if he should say anything at all. But simply being in the home of a couple of believers like Jim and Mary gave him a sense that he ought to say something, if only for form's sake.

So, gazing up, he said, almost silently, "God, if you're up there, thank you."

He relaxed back in the chair, realizing he had made a proactive choice to pray. It was a small step, but he had started a new relationship with God.

Just then, Mary wandered past the door. She was stunned to see him sitting in the chair, and then let out a whoop. "Woo-hoo!" she called out. "Praise God! Hallelujah! God is good!"

Peter cringed at her display of overt enthusiasm, and at the same time, he felt somewhat jealous of her ability to praise God in no uncertain terms. Maybe this would come too.

"Look at you!" Mary exclaimed. "I'm so happy! What happened?"

Peter found himself somewhat embarrassed to be recounting something as simple as getting out of bed and walking to the bathroom, but he understood that, under the circumstances, his trek was probably something of a small miracle, something beyond luck.

"I leaned over to see what time it was," he explained, "and then I realized I could move. So I got up. I made it a little way down the hall, all by myself."

"Aren't you special!" Mary crowed, and they both laughed. "Guess you won't need my help anymore!"

"I'm not so sure about that," Peter admitted. "I'm still pretty wrung out from taking my first steps after the accident. But I'll tell you: It feels great.

"Is Jim running the snowblower?" he asked.

Mary nodded. "It warmed up enough," she began, "so some of the snow melted and he was able to open the garage door. The good news is that we can see where the road would be. The bad news is that there's still four feet of snow on it. We're not exactly priority one in the county, since we're so isolated."

"And here I thought you were only a couple minutes from the airport," Peter said, shaking his head at the memory.

"Nowhere near it," Mary said. "I want to go out and holler at Jim and let him know the good news. Sit tight."

"That's about all I was planning on doing," Peter said.

Mary went out, and a few moments later, Peter heard the engine on the snowblower cutting out. A few moments later, Jim came bounding into the room. "Isn't that amazing?" he exclaimed, still in his parka and boots. "As I live and breathe! God is good!"

Peter noted the omitted hallelujah, which was just as well. For someone like Peter, Jim and Mary's overt declarations of belief were still a little over the top somehow.

"How should we celebrate?" Mary asked. "More bacon and eggs? Or maybe biscuits and gravy to celebrate the happy occasion?"

"Biscuits and gravy sound great," Peter agreed. He tried to stand again, but his legs simply didn't have the strength.

"I've got a cane in the garage," Jim said. "It was my dad's. I'd love for you to use it, until you get your strength back."

Peter winced at the idea that he needed a cane, but that was a heck of a lot better than remaining immobilized in bed.

"Sure," he agreed, and Jim went off to the garage to retrieve it.

"The kitchen's four steps up," Mary said. "Jim can help you get up the steps. It'll be a lot more pleasant for you to be on the main level of the house instead of trapped down here in the bedroom. How does that sound?"

"Sounds like a plan," Peter acknowledged. A minute later, Jim brought Peter the cane and led him gently down the hall. Mary took his other arm, and, together, she and Jim helped Peter to the kitchen.

"This really is a beautiful house," Peter said, casting an expert eye on the kitchen fixtures, the drawer handles, the skylights, the appliances, and all the other details that made for a well-designed high-end home. "Somebody really knew what he was doing."

Jim laughed. "We like it," he said. "Although, to tell you the truth, you could probably tell us more about why we like it than what we know. You're the expert."

"There's a sense of harmony here," Peter said. "Everything works together—all the design elements. It just feels like everything fits. That's not easy to do. Most designers don't get it right. Your guy did."

"We could go religious on you," Mary said as she opened the fridge and started pulling ingredients out, "and we could say that the whole universe is that way. But maybe you want some coffee before we get into our daily theology discussions."

"A cup of coffee would go down great right now," Peter said. "Now that I'm a free man!"

They all laughed, and Mary poured coffee all around. Jim slipped out of his outdoor clothes and poured some orange juice for Peter as Mary started making breakfast.

"Any word on when we're going to get sprung?" Peter asked.

"Not really," Jim said. "But I wouldn't be surprised if we got some good news today. We had a pretty warm twenty-four hours, and that makes a big difference when you've got this much snow."

Mary nodded. "I told Peter," she began, "that we're at the bottom of the priority list for the county, since we live so far from anything important, and there are no other families down in this valley. But they get here eventually."

Peter sipped his coffee and nodded.

"It's amazing that you don't value what you have until it's gone," he said. "Getting up and walking to the kitchen was never that big a deal. It is now."

Jim nodded. "Appreciation is the key to happiness," he said. "If you're not happy with what you've got now, it's not like something else is going to make you happy."

"Well, in that case," Peter said, grinning, "I guess I'll be on my way!"

"Not so fast," Mary said, laughing. "First, breakfast. Then we'll see what happens next."

"I'll always be glad we sprung for the generators," Jim said as Mary shaped the dough for the biscuits and put them in the oven. "Mary nearly talked me out of it. But I didn't let her!" He winked at Peter.

Mary turned around. "Actually, Mr. Big Spender," she began, chiding, "it was the other way around." She turned to Peter. "He said we could just make fires in the fireplace if it ever snowed that much. He said it would be romantic. *Please.* I said I wasn't having any of that. I'm glad I won that argument."

"You've won every argument," Jim said, and everyone laughed.

As she began to heat up the gravy, Mary asked, "Do you think you are ready to tell us the rest of the story?"

"No," Peter said, "but I guess you're entitled to hear it all since we are in this deep."

20

LET GOD
DEFEND YOU

ONCE MONDAY MORNING FINALLY ARRIVED, it was time for Peter meet his fate at an offsite coffee meeting with Digby Hunsacker. He suited up for battle, donning his best slacks, a crisp white shirt, smart shoes, and a belt that matched, ready for whatever was in store for him.

As he left the house, he kissed Catherine goodbye. She said, "Remember, all you have to do is glorify God."

Peter said, "Catherine, how am I supposed to glorify God when all I want to do is stick a fork in this guy's neck?"

"Peter, today you're going to be challenged. But your job is not to defend yourself. Your job is to glorify God. Let God defend you. That's His job. All you have to do is have faith." She gave him a knowing glance. "Now go be Christ's man. You've got this."

The coffee shop was only a five-minute drive. Peter was still on a high from the pep talk Catherine had given him. Could he do this? Would they really be okay? At this point, he didn't have much to stand on. Faith was the most solid thing he had at this point.

He entered the coffee shop more calmly than he expected, spotting Digby at a table by the window. Of course, his boss was already there, lying in wait for his prey. They exchanged pleasantries, and Digby got down to business, making quick work of his task. Perhaps he had a tee time. "Peter, I can either fire you, or you can resign."

No explanation. No opportunity for any questions or a discussion. *Behave. Glorify God.* Peter offered his resignation. Faith was all he had. Digby droned on about how they would still be friends and how this was just business—nothing personal.

Peter only heard half of what Digby was saying. But his calm demeanor was waning. He had too many questions. What about severance? What about his projects? How would his team react? A whole list of details on the other side of "resigning" filled Peter's head, stirring up anxiety in him. Perhaps faith only offered temporary solace.

Where is the exit? How do I escape this fiasco? he wondered.

He noticed something out of the corner of his eye, someone he knew. A man across the room, his back to Peter, was pouring cream into his coffee. The man was unmistakable even from behind—tall, lanky, bookish, the epitome of peace and tranquility. It was Pastor Woody, the man who had married Peter and Catherine and baptized all three of their children. For all intents and purposes, he was their family's pastor.

Pastor Woody strode directly toward Peter and Digby. Peter wondered how he was going to make the introduction. Without saying a word, the pastor sat down at the table directly behind Peter. He was only three feet away, but apparently, he hadn't noticed Peter.

Even though they hadn't acknowledged each other, Pastor Woody's presence at Peter's back calmed him as he and Digby worked through the details. A wave of peace flowed over him from behind, like the sun warming his back. Peter felt it now—the faith Catherine accessed so easily. He knew he'd be okay.

Shortly thereafter, Digby stood rather abruptly. Peter mirrored his action.

Squared off, Digby patted Peter on the shoulder and said, "Goodbye, Peter. I'll see you around."

This was his chance. A fork to the neck. It was now or never. But he didn't feel angry anymore. He chose to glorify God and wished Hunsacker well. For now, they were just words. His heart would have to catch up.

When Digby was gone, Peter just stood there, pondering. What had just happened? He was simultaneously angry and at peace. Then he turned toward Pastor Woody and waited for his attention.

After a few seconds, Woody looked up. "Peter, good to see you," he said.

"Woody, great to see you too," Peter responded. "How are you?"

"I'm well. Thanks for asking. How are you?" Woody offered, the epitome of calm and peaceful. It was just what Peter needed.

"Well, I'm fine I guess, but I have a question for you. I'm curious. Do you always come to this coffee shop?" Peter asked.

"You know, I do have a Monday morning coffee routine. I like to get a good start on my week with a little quiet time, to start the week in the word. It keeps me close to God so my heart doesn't wander toward earthly things as much."

Who talks like that? Peter asked himself. *He's so peaceful. Grounded. Holy.*

"I like to go to coffee shops," Woody added, "but I change it up every week. I don't think I have been to this one in about two years or so. Why do you ask?"

Was this luck or God? Peter thought. *Coincidence or a small miracle?*

Peter began to tell Woody the entire story. After hearing all the details, the chance encounter didn't seem to surprise Woody at all. Peter was puzzled by that but grateful he was there.

21

BREAKFAST WITH A SIDE OF FORGIVENESS

PETER'S FACE REDDENED as he reached the end of his story. He couldn't recall whether he had ever told anyone besides Catherine. Telling it now forced him to relive the entire episode, rekindling a slow rage spurred on by the humiliation. But Peter had forgotten about the warmth and peace of Pastor Woody's presence.

Jim gently touched Peter's shoulder, bringing him back to the present moment.

"Are you all right?" Mary asked.

"I think so. It's just hard to tell the story. It's so humiliating. I don't know what to do with it all," Peter confessed.

"I get that, but I love that story. It's the greatest," Jim exclaimed with a huge smile on his face.

"What?" Peter said. He thought this was another sarcastic dad joke. Bad timing and poor delivery on Jim's part. His seeming insensitivity shocked Peter.

"Peter, God loves you so much that he sent your pastor to you at the exact moment you needed him. That's a miracle. For him to not see you initially and sit down directly behind you—whoa! God had your back. Literally. That's amazing."

Peter absorbed what Jim was saying, regrouping after he realized Jim was serious. He hadn't considered the situation that way before. "It was nice," he conceded.

"Nice? Was the parting of the Red Sea nice?" Jim playfully chided. "This is a full-blown hand-of-God sighting. I'm so glad you had that experience."

"Now you're just cuckoo," Peter said. "You're missing the point. I got fired—in public, by the man I trusted most in the world at that time."

"Respectfully, I might suggest *you* are missing the point. God is tapping you on the shoulder to invite you to the freedom offered by forgiveness," Jim said gently.

"You bet. I've been waiting for Digby to apologize, to ask for my forgiveness," Peter exclaimed.

"Peter, you don't have to wait for him to apologize," Mary offered. "Forgiveness is your choice."

Perplexed, Peter said, "But why? Why should I forgive him? It's not like I did anything wrong. Digby fired me out of nowhere, for no reason. He turned my life upside down on a whim."

"Being a balanced person," Jim explained, "does not mean going through life with a chip on both shoulders. There comes a point where you just have to let go and say, 'Okay, things happen, and I can move on.'"

"What are you talking about?" Peter asked, amazed. "He takes my job for no reason and I have to forgive him? I'd rather spit on his grave!"

"He's not the only one," Mary said softly. "Your father. Digby. Eddy, for not giving you the deal. Eddy's wife. Your wife, for reaching out to Eddy. It sounds like you have a whole bunch of people who could use a little forgiveness."

"I don't get it," Peter said frankly. "Shouldn't *they* have to apologize to me?

Digby did this to me! I didn't do anything to him. Where I come from, if you don't apologize, you aren't forgiven. It's that simple."

Jim nodded. "And how's that working for you?" he asked. "I mean, where has that gotten you?"

Peter was silent.

"I'll tell you where it's gotten you," Mary said gently, "at the risk of stating the obvious. Virtually immobile, stuck in a house with two crazy strangers. That's where the whole thing has taken you. Am I wrong?"

"You two *are* crazy," Peter said, astonished at this latest display of "Christian love" that he just could not accept. "I'm waiting for Digby to apologize to me. And all of them! You've got it backward. And this whole tough love routine you are pressing on me, it's not working."

Mary and Jim stared at him almost expressionless, as though they almost welcomed his rant. Peter couldn't figure it out.

"How long have you been waiting? How long are you prepared to wait for his apology? Do you think it will ever come? What's your next move?" asked Mary.

"So, what's the point?" Peter asked, bewildered. "Is that what being a *good* Christian means—forgiving all these people for what they did to me when they don't even feel bad about it? That's a pretty lousy deal."

"What's the worst that could happen?" Jim said. "I don't think it'll kill you."

"You must be kidding," Peter spluttered.

"I kid a lot, but not right now," Jim replied.

"Not forgiving people," Mary explained, "is like taking poison and waiting for the other person to die. It's not going to hurt you to let go of these resentments and start—"

"Lady, you don't know what hurt is," Peter interrupted.

Mary was silent.

Jim leaned forward as if to defend her, but he relaxed. "Since you are asking," he said, "the Bible does have a thing or two to say about forgiveness."

"Really?" Peter asked sarcastically. "I think I know exactly what you're referring to."

"Tell me, O wise one," Jim said, with his own dose of sarcasm.

"The whole 'forgive not just seven times but seventy times seven' thing. That's what you are talking about, right?"

"Matthew 18 is what you are referring to, Peter," Jim said.

"Yeah, Matthew 18 or whatever. It is like the billy club of apologies. I've seen that movie plenty of times. It doesn't work. It just breeds resentment and broken relationships at the hands of some self-righteous religious do-gooders," Peter said.

"Peter?" Mary said. She waited for him to make eye contact with her.

Peter turned his head and locked eyes with her.

"I'm sorry for what others in the church have done to you," she said, with complete sincerity. "Will you forgive me on their behalf?"

This caught Peter off guard. He attempted to speak. What he wanted to tell her was that he hadn't been hurt by others. That she didn't need to apologize on their behalf. But he couldn't. It was as if his lips were sealed. He could not speak. All the while, his brain was processing what she'd said. It transmitted a signal directly to his heart. He found himself softening even beyond his own resolve to hate those who had wronged him. Then, suddenly, he said, "Yes."

He said it so definitively that even the most jaded and skeptical side of him believed the word he had just uttered. He felt a rush of peace wash over his whole body.

"Thank you," she said tenderly.

Jim chimed in. "Peter, I wasn't actually going to mention Matthew 18 to you. That was not what I was thinking, but obviously, that little exchange was a powerful step in the process to forgive others who have wronged you."

Peter acknowledged the significance of the past few minutes by nodding.

"I want to share with you the concept of loving your enemies," Jim continued in a soft voice. "'If they are thirsty, give them something to drink.

If they are hungry, give them something to eat. By doing so, you will heap burning coals on their head. Do not overcome evil by evil. Overcome evil by good.'"

"About the only thing I like in what you just said," Peter joked, infusing a little humor, "is heaping burning coals on their head. Let's start a fire!"

"I figured that might be the phrase you would like," Jim said. "The verse goes on to say that we are not to avenge ourselves but leave that to God. So, if God is smarter than us, we should defer to His wisdom even when it doesn't make sense to us or feel like the intuitive thing to do.

"The world judges us by our actions," he continued, "but we judge ourselves by our intentions. In other words, we're always giving ourselves a break but never the other guy. Maybe it's time to try a different approach."

Peter sighed. "You've got me at a disadvantage," he said. "First of all, you're both right. I mean, that's obvious. And second, you know the Bible better than I do. And it's not like I can just get up and leave because I don't like what you're telling me. I've got to take some time to think about it."

"I wouldn't think about it for too long," Jim said, getting up. "Just decide to forgive, and forgive. Your heart will catch up. In the meantime, maybe you can start going through a mental list of people who need forgiving."

"I'd make sure God's on the list," Mary said, placing a steaming plate of smothered biscuits in front of Peter. "And I'd make sure you're on the list too. In the meantime, let's eat."

"Breakfast with a side of forgiveness," Peter said, resigned to what they were telling him. "I guess that's what's on the menu."

SATURDAY

22

COFFEE AND
A CALLING

PETER HAD A FITFUL NIGHT OF SLEEP. He tossed and turned, awaking before dawn. Relatively mobile now, he made his way to the kitchen, following the smell of coffee. No lights were on, and no one else seemed to be up. The coffeepot was steaming, and he could see that it was set to automatically brew to awaken everyone with the aroma of fresh coffee. These two—they thought of everything.

He grabbed a mug, poured himself a cup, and took a seat at the breakfast table. The whole episode with Digby—the firing, forgiveness—was present on his mind. But Peter couldn't come to grips with extending the gift of forgiveness to the man who had betrayed him. Peter had the moral upper hand.

Taking a sip of coffee, it was just the right level of bitterness to match his feelings. Digby should come crawling to him, begging for his forgiveness. His former boss needed to humble himself before Peter.

Then Peter stopped midsip. A thought hit him like a ton of bricks. He lowered the mug, wiped his mouth, and pursed his lips.

Humble himself.

Peter closed his eyes and shook his head slowly. How could he be so arrogant? How could he be so self-righteous? That's what Jim and Mary had been saying all along in a very polite way. *Humble yourself. Extend the hand of forgiveness even to those who aren't humble enough to ask for it.*

Jim's comment from the day before echoed in his head: *Don't take too much time thinking. Just decide to forgive, and forgive. Your heart will catch up.*

"Maybe I can forgive him. It's certainly not my normal response," Peter said out loud.

He could hear Mary's voice in his head, *That's what forgiveness is: doing what God is inviting us to do—forgive—even when we don't feel like it. But as we take a step forward in faith, He changes our heart beyond our own understanding and our normal response. Freedom for you, Peter, is within your grasp. Forgive Digby just like God has forgiven you.*

As Peter watched the sunlight slowly begin to stream in through the window, Jim burst into the kitchen with great joy. "Let freedom ring!" he shouted. "Good morning, Peter. Good to see you up and about."

"Top of the morning to you, old chap," Peter offered in a laughable Cockney accent, attempting to return Jim's energy and air of goofiness.

Jim stopped, facing Peter, and said, "Now we are talking. I certainly don't know the old Peter, but it looks like he is feeling better and making a return to himself."

"I think so," Peter said. "Although I am not sure any of the old me is left. You all have done a number on me, and I might not ever be the same."

"Can't put new wine in an old wineskin." Jim laughed.

"So I'm sure you've got some sort of lesson plan for me today," Peter said, his tone open and interested. He could sense his time coming to a close and wanted to learn more from these two who were committed to God in a way he wished he could be.

"*Purpose,*" Jim said briskly as he poured coffee for himself and freshened Peter's cup. "I was thinking we might have a brief convo about the idea of purpose. Of what you do with your life. Or maybe a better word is *calling.*"

Peter scratched his chin. "I don't think I have a calling," he admitted. "I've just sort of fallen into everything that's come my way: football, UT, my career. It's not like I've ever heard God speaking to me about my career—do this or do that. Things have kind of just happened."

Jim nodded. "That's not what you said the other day. You reconciled your life as not having missed the turnoffs. You implied that everything has happened for a reason. So, why has design and construction happened *to you*?" Jim asked. "Let me ask it another way. Why do you go to work?"

Peter studied him, wondering if this was a trick question of some sort. "I go to work because . . ." His voice trailed off. "Because I've gotta support my family. It's how I put bread on the table."

"Of course," Jim said, calmly sipping his coffee. "Any other reasons?"

Peter thought for a moment. "Because I'm good at it? Because I like it?" He paused. "It's satisfying. You know, starting with just the plot of land that may or may not be suitable for a nice house. And then you figure out the contours of the land and what goes where and what the curb appeal will be and how you go from public spaces to increasingly private spaces. Like from the living room to the kitchen and up the stairs to the bedrooms and so on. It's like putting a puzzle together. And then you actually get to see the thing coming to fruition. It's pretty cool."

Jim set out spoons and bowls at the kitchen table, which Peter noticed with a practiced eye had been carved from first-class Carrara marble.

"Nice table," Peter commented.

"We like it," Mary said as she entered the kitchen and grabbed some coffee.

"Would you describe your work as completely satisfying?" Jim asked, probing gently.

Peter thought for a minute before he spoke. He watched Mary flick her packet of sweetener before opening it. "I don't know what you mean," he said.

"Let up on the man for a second," Mary teased Jim. "Cereal, gentlemen?" she asked. "We're low on the good stuff—blizzard and all."

Peter, grateful for the opportunity to dig in, was about to pour the milk for the cereal Mary had just put on the table when he suddenly remembered something. "I guess you guys say grace," Peter said.

"We do," Mary agreed.

"If you want to include me, feel free," Peter said.

"Do you want to lead us?"

"I would, but the only one I know is Johnny Appleseed from my camp days," Peter said.

"Wonderful. How does it go?" Mary asked.

"Well, you have to start by putting your hands over your head and making a big circle with your arms."

"Really? That's intriguing. Jim, come on. Join us. Put your arms up," Mary insisted.

Jim did as he was told.

"Then, you start the prayer," Peter said. "Ohhhhh." He drew out the word, then dropped his hands quickly as he launched into the rest of the song. "The Lord is good to me. And so I thank the Lord. For giving me the things I need, the sun and the rain and the apple seeds. The Lord is good to me. Amen."

Mary and Jim erupted into applause afterward, saying "amen" over and over again.

"We love that," Jim said.

"What about *your* prayers?" Peter asked.

Jim nodded and closed his eyes. Mary and Peter did the same.

"Dear Lord, thank you for restoring Peter's ability to walk again. You truly are mighty to save. Thank you for giving us this opportunity to be of service to him and to live out our own calling. Please help him hone his idea of what a calling really is, and thank you for the wonderful food which my beautiful wife has just prepared. In Jesus's name, amen."

Mary and Peter echoed their amens, and Peter added, "That's the most unusual grace I've ever heard," he said through a mouthful of cereal.

"Jim tailors them to the occasion," Mary explained. "They're very specific."

"So let me ask you the question again," Jim said, tucking into his breakfast. "Is there anything about your work that you don't find satisfying?"

Peter thought about it as he leaned over his bowl, slurping cereal as if he had never seen food before. He was ravenously hungry, a good sign of returning health, he guessed.

"I don't know," he admitted. "I guess there's one thing."

Jim and Mary waited.

"Everybody I work for is rich," Peter said. "And they all had nice places to live in before I got there. And if I hadn't come along, somebody else, like Digby—to name a name—would have gotten to them and built them a really super house. So it's not like I'm—I don't know—doing anything special or different for these folks."

"You're building their dream house," Mary said. "That's pretty special."

"I guess," Peter said. "But the houses these people had before the one I built were pretty much dream houses already. It's not like they were moving out of a basement apartment to a penthouse. They're typically moving from a four-thousand-square-foot house into an eight-thousand-square-foot house. They are starting with so much and then building more of the same."

"Be that as it may," Jim said, "you are doing something that you love to do and that they will appreciate."

"I guess," Peter said. "I never really thought about it that much."

"So, what you're doing," Jim interpreted, "is satisfying from an aesthetic standpoint. But from a sense of serving others, it kind of leaves you wanting."

Peter bit his lip. "I never thought about it that way," he admitted. "I guess I've tried never to think about it at all in that perspective. But it's true. It's just not something I . . . It's just not something that . . . I mean, it's provided a good living for us, which is great. And I'm grateful. Don't get me wrong. But if you said to me that when I'm lying on my deathbed and my legacy is a thousand eight-thousand-square-foot houses that ultimately got knocked down to build twelve-thousand-square-foot houses, I guess I'd be like, 'What was the point?'"

"And that's the difference," Jim said gently, "between a profession and a calling. You're a builder by profession. But a calling may mean more than a job."

Peter thought about Jim's words and nodded. "There's a guy named Phillip Johnson," he said. "An architect. He was a giant in our field, almost like a Frank Lloyd Wright. And when he turned eighty-two, someone asked him why he didn't retire. And he said something like, 'Why should I retire and build castles on the beach when I can still build buildings in the real world?' So in that sense, I relate, because I enjoy the work.

"But is building and designing something I feel called to do? I'm not sure. I'm not even really sure I know what a calling is. I do know that I have stalled out professionally."

Neither Jim nor Mary spoke. They sensed, correctly, that Peter had more he wanted to express.

23

GOOD LUCK
CHARM

"WHEN I GRADUATED HIGH SCHOOL," he began, his
voice rising as if asking a question, "my dad showed up—out of the blue. I
hadn't seen him for probably five years at that point. He hadn't been to a single
one of my football games. But for whatever reason, he was at my graduation.
My mother was glad he was there for me, but their relationship was strained.

"I invited him to the party we were going to have afterward to celebrate,
even though I sensed my mother was worried for me. But he is my dad, and
I wanted to. And he had shown up. So I invited him.

"He could tell my mom was hurt, and he didn't want to make her uncomfortable, and he probably didn't want me to be uncomfortable either. He gave
me a briefcase for my graduation present—right after the ceremony. I was
still standing there in my cap and gown, and now I'm walking around with
this briefcase. It was really more like a satchel. All the other kids were like,
'Hey, what happened? You just get a job?'

"But I loved that briefcase, because it was like my father saying to me, *I
believe in you. I believe you can do something in this world—not just with your*

hands but with your head too. I really treasured it. And, I mean, I could go out now and buy a super high-end briefcase or satchel or whatever you want to call it. But I stuck with this one for my whole career. I always figured it was my good luck charm. Whenever I took it with me to close a deal, I got the deal."

No one was eating anymore. Mary and Jim were rapt, listening to Peter's words.

"It was also a conversation starter. People would say, 'What's the deal with that old, battered briefcase?' I would tell them some sort of story that would satisfy them while turning the conversation to their favorite subject: themselves. They would launch into a similar story. And before you know it, we were closing the deal.

"And then one day, I couldn't find it. My wife had always been on my case to get rid of it and get something nicer, because it was so beat-up. Plus, it looked like it had come from a five-and-dime, and it probably had. She swore up and down she hadn't tossed it. You know how wives like to throw things out. No offense, Mary. But it's like a wife thing. If they think their husbands should upgrade, they don't ask; they just toss.

"But she would have sworn on a stack of Bibles that she hadn't thrown it out. So I went to Neimans and I bought a new case. It was nice—high end, beautiful leather, expensive. But it wasn't the same. That's around the time I went into my tailspin. I lost eight great deals. Digby got them all. There I was with my fancy briefcase, walking in with contracts to close and walking out with them unsigned.

"It was a run of really bad luck; at least that's what I thought at the time. And then a week before I was coming out to see Eddy, I found it—the old satchel. It was in the garage, stashed under my golf clubs. I guess I had tossed it there without thinking one day, and it never occurred to me to look there. I was so happy. I thought, *I've got my briefcase back. It's my lucky charm. I've got my mojo back. I'm going to go to Taos and everything's going to change.*

"Well, everything changed, all right. But not the way I planned."

24

FATHERS'
BLESSINGS

THEY SAT IN SILENCE for a long time after Peter concluded his story.

"Where's the case now?" Jim asked gently.

"Up the hill, at Eddy's," Peter admitted. "When I stormed out of there, I forgot it. I felt super embarrassed and foolish. When I realized I had left it, I rationalized that the thing is worth only ten cents anyway. If I had remembered it, all those guys who are practically billionaires probably would have just been laughing at me while I was standing there waiting for it. My ten-cent lucky charm."

"You know, your mojo has nothing to do with that briefcase," Mary said softly. "That satchel was a gift from your dad. It's clear you love him."

Peter nodded.

"And he loves you, despite the challenges in your relationship," Mary added. "He showed his love for you with that gift, even though he might not have had the words."

"Peter, your father gave you what every son wants," Jim said.

Peter was laser focused on Jim. He had his full attention.

"He gave you his blessing. Whether you knew it or not, you had to find that satchel because that is your earthly father's blessing, given to you in the only way he could communicate it. But he gave it to you."

Peter's jaw dropped open. He could feel something that he couldn't do anything about. He was stunned. A hole in his heart immediately sealed. In place of an empty pit, his heart was overflowing with the grace Jim was offering.

"This is no lucky charm. This is your father's blessing. And now it is time to step into your heavenly father's blessing," Jim said, fervently pulling Peter out of his momentary trance.

"What's that?" Peter stammered.

"The gifts he has given to you for the calling He has prepared for you."

"I know," Peter admitted. "God didn't want me to have those deals for whatever reason. I just wish He could've divided them up among a bunch of other builders. He didn't have to give them all to Digby."

Mary and Jim laughed.

Peter paused and thought for a moment. "My gifts?"

"Yes. Your gifts. Look how God has used you for the things you think you are not good at: praying with your grandmother, fundraising for the camp, glorifying God when you want to assault Digby with a fork. Imagine what you might be able to do with the gifts He has given you in abundance: your intellect, your eye for design, your client bedside manner, and your business acumen."

"Okay. I get it. How do I turn my profession into a calling?" Peter asked.

"Are you a good builder?" Jim asked.

"I am," Peter said truthfully, and as objectively and humbly as he could.

"If you are a good builder, why do you think you didn't get those jobs you believe you were perfectly suited for?"

"My heart wasn't in it," Peter blurted out, as if something or someone had taken over his body and made him utter those words.

"Now we're talking," Jim said. "You've said you like designing and building homes," Jim said, summarizing what Peter had told him previously, "but the part that you're questioning is the audience—who you're designing the homes for?"

Peter nodded. "I guess that sums it up," he said.

"So maybe if you were designing homes for different people," Jim suggested, "maybe the right people, the whole thing might mean more to you."

"Like who?" Peter asked, his tone sarcastic. "The homeless?"

Jim shrugged. "Sounds good to me," he said.

"The homeless can't afford what I do," Peter said. "Anyway, what's a guy from the street gonna do with an eight-thousand-square-foot McMansion—bring all his friends over and have a party?"

"Hold that thought for a minute. We might come back to that," Jim said.

After that, neither Jim nor Mary spoke. They waited for Peter as he stared back at them.

"I hate when you do this," Peter said, embarrassed. "Sounds like you're waiting for me to solve my own problem."

"We think you already did," Jim said gently.

"What do you mean?" Peter asked.

"Have you ever thought of your business as a ministry?" Mary asked.

"I run a for-profit business," Peter told her.

"I assumed that. Running your business as a ministry doesn't require you to be a nonprofit. You can serve God while serving your for-profit clients," Jim said.

"I'm not following you," Peter confessed.

"God calls us to go make disciples of Jesus Christ," Mary said.

"The Great Commission," Peter exclaimed as he pretended to push an invisible buzzer sitting on the table.

"Right you are, Mr. Christiansen," Jim barked in his game show voice. "Bonus points for you if you make it to the lightning round."

Mary smirked at the boys' exchange.

"The word *go*," Jim continued, "is translated to mean 'as you are going.' Meaning, you are to do your discipleship, your ministry, as you live your life. It doesn't require you necessarily to stop doing your work and then go on a mission trip. Those who are called as businesspeople have a mission field where their businesses are planted."

"I do really like running a business, leading people, building the infrastructure of the business like I build the homes I design," Peter shared.

"Who is your mission field, Peter?" Jim asked.

"Great question," Peter said.

"What about Derek Martland, your Bible study guide?" Mary offered.

"He already has a home," Peter offered, a little confused.

"Sure. What I meant was, what about homeowners like Derek Martland? He used his house as a church, right?"

"Yes. He did. He even had a sign on the front door letting everyone know that he loved Jesus," Peter said excitedly.

"Why not find those clients who are like him?" Mary asked. "People who are using their resources to create spaces to be used by God to minister to His people?"

"I'm blown away," Peter said. "I have never thought about my business this way. I've only thought about it through the lens of the Hunsacker firm. As a result, I've been focused on serving the Trishes of the world. That's who I served at the Hunsacker firm. That's who has been referred to me."

Mary got up and rushed out of the room, as if on a mission.

"Sounds like you might have just found the start of a calling," Jim said approvingly.

Peter scratched his chin. "You think?" he asked, looking thoughtfully at Jim. "Maybe I did."

Mary popped back in with something in her hand. As she sat back down, she slid it across the marble table. The book came to rest perfectly positioned directly in front of Peter.

"Pick it up. Thumb through it," Mary said, inviting Peter to get his hands on his new gift.

"There is nothing in here," Peter exclaimed, a little confused. "The pages are blank."

"I know. How great is that?" Mary said, as if Peter knew what she was referring to. "This is the start of your vision, your calling. Journal your conversations with God as He speaks to you. Review this journal, and I bet your calling will emerge right from these very pages—these currently blank pages calling out to you."

"Wow. Thank you. I'm not big on journaling," Peter confessed as he thumbed through the pages, half hoping to find something—anything—already written that might give him a head start.

"Peter, I'm in your camp," Jim said, smiling. "I'm not big on journaling either. But when I was in the military, I found it to be an incredible experience. God's voice spoke to me. I wrote what I thought I heard Him tell me. Only after the fact did I see the brilliance in His messages to me over time. The scribblings allowed me to discern His voice versus mine."

"I'll give it a shot. What do I have to lose?" Peter conceded.

"You have everything to gain!" Mary offered, championing the cause. "Write the vision plain on tablets so that he who runs may read it," she added with a little extra flair, as if to punctuate her wisdom.

"Jim, let's skedaddle. Leave him to his conversations with God."

Jim and Mary left Peter with his new gift to ponder the future of his calling, his ministry in the business world. Stepping out of his comfort zone. Saying yes to God.

At that moment, the phone rang.

"Sounds like the phone lines are back up," Mary said, picking up the receiver.

"I'll go check the generators," Jim said as he rose from the table and exited out the back door.

"Yes," Mary said into the phone. "Thank you for letting me know. I'll call you later." She replaced the receiver on its cradle.

Jim came back in, shaking snow from his boots and announced, "We've got power!"

"I can call my wife," Peter exclaimed. "I guess I could say . . . um . . . hallelujah?"

Jim and Mary laughed.

"Nobody's forcing you to." Mary smiled.

"Hallelujah," Peter said, tentatively at first, but he found he liked the sound of the word coming from his mouth. "Let me try that again, with a little more emphasis. *Hallelujah!*"

25

GRACE
AND MERCY

"I CAN'T BELIEVE I CAN FINALLY CALL HOME!"
Peter said again. "Do you mind if I use the phone? I just gotta talk to
Catherine! She's got to be worried sick."

"Absolutely," Jim exclaimed. "And then the second call will be to the sheriff, to let them know you are here in one piece. I'm sure everybody wondered
what happened to you after the party."

Peter thought for a moment. "You're right," he said, sidling up to the
kitchen counter. "I never even thought about that. Do you think Eddy's been
worried about me?"

"I don't see why not," Mary replied. "You leave a man's house in a roar-
ing blizzard and nobody hears from you again. Since you went down the
wrong road, they probably wouldn't have associated the broken guardrails
you crashed through with your accident. Anyway, we'll call the sheriff after you
call Catherine."

Mary handed Peter the phone, which felt clunky and old-fashioned. It
didn't matter. He was overjoyed. He dialed his wife's cell.

It had barely begun to ring when Catherine picked up. "Hello?" she said, with a voice that betrayed deep concern.

An unknown area code and a missing husband will do that to you, Peter thought.

"Honey, it's me!" he said softly into the handset. "I'm okay! I'm alive!"

Jim and Mary slid out of the room to give him some privacy.

"Did you hear that?" he asked restlessly. "I'm alive! I'm fine! I had a terrible accident, but these really nice people saved me and took care of me, and we just got power and phone service back!"

He didn't hear any words on the other end of the line, but Catherine began to sob uncontrollably.

"Honey, it's okay," he said soothingly, but words would have no effect. How could they?

"Oh, Peter," Catherine finally said through tears, "we feared the worst. Especially . . ." Her voice was heaving with sobs. "Especially when we didn't hear anything for so long. We didn't know what had happened. Are you really okay?"

"It's unbelievable," he said excitedly. "I didn't break a bone in my body, I don't think. I guess I'd know. These really nice people have been taking care of me. She was a nurse. They're like angels. Maybe they *are* angels. Who knows? Anyway, I'm fine. I've been so worried that I couldn't get through to you."

"Why couldn't you call?" Catherine said, regaining a bit of control over her voice. Peter heard some shuffling in the background, and Catherine's voice was slightly muffled, like her hand was over the phone. "Daddy's calling! He's okay. He's alive! We're gonna see him again!" And now Peter could hear the children shouting, and Catherine started crying all over again. He couldn't make out a word anyone was saying.

Finally, Catherine got back on the line. "Where are you?" she asked.

"It's miraculous. I don't know how else to put it. Anyway, we've been snowed in this whole time. We still are. We're in a valley. No service. This is the first moment we just got power back, so there was no way I could call."

"When are you coming home?" Catherine asked. "We've been so scared! I haven't slept in days! None of us have!"

Peter sighed, feeling a terrible kind of guilt for all he'd put his family through, all because of his reckless decision to leave the party and head out into the blizzard.

"I'm so sorry," he said. "It's all my fault. I'll explain when I see you."

"None of that matters," Catherine said insistently. "All I care about is when you're coming home!" Grace, mercy—she was amazing.

"As soon as they plow the roads here," he said. "We're gonna call the sheriff right now. Maybe they'll do something to get me out of here."

"You sure you're okay?" Catherine asked, and her tone indicated that she barely believed this was happening, that Peter was, in fact, safe.

"I'm perfectly fine," Peter insisted. "I was definitely shaken up, but I'm getting better every day. I'll call you as soon as I know when they can rescue me from here. But in the meantime, I'm with this wonderful couple. Also, guess what! When I get back, we're going to church! I can't wait to thank God in person!"

Catherine laughed. "I'm happy you want to go to church," she said, "and we will! But you don't need to be in church to thank God in person!"

Peter thought for a moment about his caregivers. "To tell you the truth," he said quietly, "I think I already have. Listen, I've gotta get off the phone. They need to call the sheriff. You're the first call we made. Of course."

"Love you so much, honey," Catherine said. "Call back so you can talk to the kids."

"As soon as we call the sheriff," Peter said. "Believe me, I just want to come home! I can't wait to see you again! I think things are going to be a lot different when I get home. Love you!"

"Love you so much!" Catherine exclaimed, and they disconnected.

26

THE FAVOR

JIM AND MARY CAME BACK into the room.

"I'll call the sheriff," Jim said quietly. "I guess your wife was pretty happy to hear from you."

"You could say that," Peter said. He moved away from the phone so Jim would have space.

Jim dialed 911. "Hey, it's Jim, out in Coyote Valley . . . Yeah, we just got service restored. Listen, the man who was in the truck accident last week—he went through the guardrails on Route 114—we've got him! He's here, he survived, he's fine, and he wants to go home. Any chance we can get some snowplows out this way? . . . That's tremendous," he said. "Very grateful. Yes, he called his wife. You'll call Eddy? That's great. You might mention that he's due for a new truck." He hung up.

"They're working the plows all day," Jim said, laughing. "Just as soon as they finish plowing some of the other roads, they will get to us—most likely by tomorrow at the latest."

"I can't thank the two of you enough," Peter said, "for everything you've done for me. This is unbelievable. How can I ever repay you?"

"Pass it on," Mary said, smiling. "That's how it works. We're all God's kids doing His work as He calls us to it. The key is to say yes whenever He asks."

Peter thought about that for a moment in light of his new perspective on using his business as part of his calling, his mission to serve people on behalf of God.

"We overheard you tell Catherine," Jim began delicately, "that you thought things would be different when you returned home. If you don't mind us asking, what did you mean by that?"

"You've both given me a lot to think about this week. I've been absorbing as best I can. I hope I can remember it all."

"Just write it in your journal, and you will have it forever," Mary said.

Peter smiled. "What I'm getting at is that I don't really feel like my time with you is complete. Don't get me wrong, I'm catching the first snowplow out of here. But I think something is missing."

"What's that?" Jim asked.

"Well, it requires an ask—asking God's kids doing His work, as you say. Are you up for one last favor for your favorite hostage—I mean guest?"

"Of course, we—" Mary started.

Jim interrupted. "Depends on what it is, ol' pal."

"Now that I know I am going home," Peter said, "in order to go forward, I've got to go back."

Jim was perplexed. "Well," he began, "if you've accused us of confusing you this week, turnabout is fair play. I'm totally lost! Tell us what you mean."

"I've got to go back to the crash site," Peter said firmly. "I have to see it for myself."

"That's not a good idea," Mary said, furrowing her brow and extending her hand as if to keep him from flying through the front windshield. "Plus your health. You might not be up for the physical exertion."

Peter turned to Jim, who caught his gaze. Peter tried to convey that he needed to see the crash site, that it was part of the healing process. He wondered if Jim's background in the military would make him understand.

Mary glanced back and forth between them. "Peter Jonathan Christiansen, I am your nurse," she said firmly. "I rescued you. I have taken care of you for seven days. You may not go. In the words of your mom, I have just two words for you: *Behave!*"

After her speech, she shook her head. Jim was trying to hide a smirk. She brushed her palms together, washing her hands of any involvement in this crazy idea. As she turned away, she said, "Well, what do you need me to do to make this ridiculous scheme successful?"

"Are you sure you want to do this, Peter?" Jim asked.

"I have to do it," Peter responded emphatically.

"A grand adventure," Mary exclaimed sarcastically. "As if we haven't had enough drama in this house the past week, let's add some more."

Her good-natured ribbing kept her opinion of the entire mission front and center while also lightening the mood. Peter hadn't even noticed that he felt nervous to return to the wreckage.

"Remember," she said, "all successful projects start with prayer and good music."

They prayed. They played good music and worked out their plan to hike to the crash site the following morning, before the roads were cleared and Peter could be taken to Eddy's before the long journey home.

"Well, that makes sense and sounds good to me," Jim said. "We can do this. Why don't we take a break and you call home again to talk to your kids. Would that be okay?"

Peter turned to Mary for approval.

"Have at it!" she said.

Jim paused and then said, "Once you're done with that call, what if we called your friend Eddy? To see if he's got some aircraft standing by that can take you home?"

Peter's face clouded. "I don't really know if I want to talk to Eddy right now," he said.

And then a thought crossed his mind. "Actually, that would be a great idea. Let Eddy know that if he's still in town, I'd like to see him."

"He's still here," Jim said confidently.

Peter was puzzled.

"Call your kids," Jim said.

"I would love that. It was great to talk to Catherine. But I can't wait to talk to my kids!" Peter said.

Jim and Mary looked at each other and grinned.

"Call your kids," Jim repeated, and he and Mary left the kitchen. "We'll be in the den. I think I fell asleep during *Casablanca* last month. I want to see how that picture turns out."

"I'll be right there," Peter said, and he turned back toward the phone for the second greatest call he would ever make in his entire life.

After twenty minutes on the line with his children, who were as overjoyed to speak with their father again as Peter was to speak with them, he joined Jim and Mary in the den and watched the last five minutes of *Casablanca*. It was the scene at the airport, where Humphrey Bogart tells Ingrid Bergman that she and her husband need to get on the airplane because they have a mission to perform.

"Well, that scene is different for me now," Peter said quietly. "I'm getting ready to get on a flight with my own mission."

SUNDAY

27

THE CRASH SITE

THE TRIO BUNDLED UP TO HEAD OUT EARLY. Even though the snowstorms had stopped a few days before, the early morning temperatures were cold. They did not know how long it would take to make the round-trip journey from Jim and Mary's house to the crash site. They wanted to pace themselves to return in time to get Peter reunited with his family.

After two hours of slow progress, Jim and Mary supporting Peter along the way, stopping to rest as needed, they finally arrived at the clearing. The Ford F-150—or what was left of it—still lay in a mangled heap where it had come to rest.

Peter felt stunned. The wreckage could not have looked more violent, rendering the vehicle unrecognizable. Snowdrifts covering parts of the wreckage made the destroyed vehicle even more menacing, like it had been chewed up and eaten by the mountainside. It was perfect destruction.

"Peter?" Jim said after a few moments.

Peter couldn't find words just yet.

"Peter?" Jim said again.

Just then Peter felt himself wobble.

Mary and Jim both tightened their grip to support him a little more firmly.

Peter mumbled something even he didn't understand.

"What did you say?" Mary asked.

"He saved me! He saved me! He saved me!" Peter said, getting louder each time he said it.

"I should be dead! No one should have walked away from this. This is complete and utter destruction! This is death! I am alive! This is a miracle by the hand of God! He saved me!"

"I chose to get behind the wheel in a snowstorm in unfamiliar terrain. I did this. I deserved to die based on this carnage."

Mary and Jim were silent.

"I've never even told you two: The worst part is that all of this could have been prevented. The man who received me at the airport and took me to the truck . . . he offered to drive me to Eddy's house. I said, 'No, I've got this.' How arrogant. How stupid. How prideful."

Jim cleared his throat as quietly as he could and said, "Peter, I know."

"You know what?" Peter asked.

"I know that your driver offered to take you to Eddy's house," Jim said. "That you could have gone to his house and been able to leave even in a snowstorm, but you declined the offer."

"How could you possibly know that?" Peter asked.

"That driver . . . was me."

"What do you mean it was you? I met you for the first time at your house the morning after you rescued me."

"Peter, you don't remember, because you barely noticed me. You were focused on other things, things I now know about."

"Impossible. How?"

"I now know that God sent me that day to take care of you. He knew you needed to get to Eddy's house. He knew the meeting would go poorly. He knew your pride would not allow you to stay at his house. He knew you would want to leave. He knew the storm was going to be bad. He sent me. I was here to help you . . ."

"And I said no to your assistance. I said no to the provision God was offering," Peter declared. "That's an unfortunate turn of events. That's a whole new set of facts I have to contend with. This might be harder than I imagined."

Mary and Jim helped him over to a rock and lowered him onto it. They backed away from him to give him some space to process.

"God, what are you doing here to me, for me, in this place?" Peter asked the cold air around him.

Nothing. There was no response.

Peter felt himself starting to slide off the rock. He caught himself and positioned himself firmly. "God, I need to know you are here, that you are for me. Tell me what to do."

Peter.

It was barely audible, a whisper through the trees. Peter chose to hear it. He chose not to question it. He said, "Yes, Lord, here I am."

Forgive.

"What? Tell me. Forgive what?" Peter asked plaintively.

Before the question left his lips, the impression in his heart was clear.

"Lord, forgive me. Forgive me for my pride, my brashness, my judgment of others. Forgive me for all that I have done to sin against you. I commit my life to you, my business to you, my family to you. All that I have is yours. Use me as you wish. Call me to service for you, and I will say yes. Give me the strength and courage to say yes."

Immediately, a feeling of peace washed over him. It transcended anything he had previously known or might ever know. His body did not ache. He felt healed, complete, whole. He felt fit for the fight to come.

He said the Lord's prayer. As he got to the part about delivering us from evil, he was struck by a sense of urgency, a quickening in his soul to grant the forgiveness he had been withholding. It sprung forth from him and flowed

like a river through the desert. *I forgive Digby, Eddy, Trish, Dad, . . . myself.*
He forgave everyone he had previously believed he had an earthly right to
hold a grudge against, everyone on whom he had been waiting to extract his
passive revenge. His transcendent peace magnified. He rested firmly in the
palm of God's hand.

Peter felt an impression from the Lord deep in his heart, a tender message, "Peter, I did not demand your life on that night. Knowing you would
give it to me is all that I ask. Get up. Dust yourself off and let's get to work."

28

A GIFT
AND GOODBYE

THE TREK BACK TO THE HOUSE was physically easier, but Peter had little memory of it. It was a blur of warmth and calm, the sun of God's love melting the snow on his heart. Resting in his room, Jim's study, he heard a tap on the door.

"Come in," he said.

Jim walked in, a little more solemn than his typical self.

"Someone die?" Peter joked.

"Not yet," Jim responded, keeping pace with Peter's newfound humor. "I'm checking on you. You had quite the experience at the crash site this morning."

"That I did. It was profound," Peter shared. "I'm ready to go home. I have everything I came here to find. I didn't even know I was searching for it."

"That's great to hear," Jim affirmed.

"I had to give up my old ways, Jim. You helped me see that. I'm trading up."

"'He is no fool who gives up what he cannot keep in order to gain what he cannot lose,'" Jim quoted.

"I was lost, all right. I think I just never had the courage before to change."

"I think you always had the courage. You just never had the time or had someone sit with you to work through it all. Discipleship of others is a hallmark of the faith. I trust that, as you work out your faith daily, you will help others do the same. Twelve apostles became a legion of believers that today number over two billion souls."

The two men took in the reality of the last statement—the impact of those who chose beyond belief to actually believe.

"Do you think you are all right after this morning? Feeling up to the next leg of the journey?" Jim asked.

"I am. In fact, as I was sitting here before you came in, I was chatting with God."

"Oh, really? Pray tell, what did the big guy have to say to you?"

"Well, it's a bit interesting. I used to think that the purpose of my life was to work hard and make a name for myself. I almost died, which would have kept me from that purpose. Then what's the purpose of my life?"

"Excellent question. Did you get an answer?" Jim asked.

"Jim, right here in this very room, God impressed upon me the following: *Peter, that night of the accident, I did not demand your life. Knowing you would give it to me is all that I ask. Get up. Dust yourself off, and let's get to work.*"

Jim stared at Peter.

"Well, aren't you going to say something?" Peter asked.

"Peter, you are not the man you were seven days ago. Through this experience, God has transformed you. He has healed you physically. He has healed you emotionally. He has healed you spiritually. In our house, we call that a miracle and get on down the road. I can't wait to see what He does in and through you for His people. I am honored to know you."

"Thank you, Jim. Thanks to you and Mary, I have everything I need for the new world."

Jim walked over to the other side of the study and reached for the sword hanging on the wall, dislodging it from the two pegs holding it in place.

He then grabbed the trowel from the wall next to the sword and turned to face Peter.

"Peter, when the Israelites came back from exile in Babylon, they were called to rebuild the walls of Jerusalem under the leadership of Nehemiah. But there were enemies that did not want them to succeed. So the men armed themselves with swords to fend off any marauders while simultaneously using a trowel for the masonry work to rebuild the wall."

"I can't wait to dig into that story more fully when I get home," Peter said gratefully. "Thank you for sharing that with me, Jim."

"I want you to have this trowel. I also worked construction as a young man. It taught me a lot about life, as I suspect it did for you. This simple instrument reminds me to build into my relationship with God and with others He places divinely in my path."

"Jim, I can't possibly take one of your prized possessions," Peter exclaimed.

"Peter, please. Be a good receiver."

"I also want you to have this sword. It was forged in Spain. It was a gift from a man named Carlos who ran a factory in Bermejo, once the capital of Spain. For over five hundred years, the Christians, Jews, and Muslims lived peacefully together. His factory produced swords for our military allies all over the world in hopes that that type of peace would be possible again someday. I worked for him one summer and never learned so much about the world and God's people in such a short time. I want you to have both."

Peter saw that failing to be an eager recipient of these amazing gifts would disappoint his hosts. He nodded and accepted them as graciously as he knew how. "Thank you, Jim. I will treasure them as a reminder of my time here and all that you and Mary have taught me."

Mary walked in. "Hey, boys. The sheriff just called," she said. "They'll plow the roads here at two o'clock. I spoke to Eddy. He said he'd have a jet to take you home anytime after five p.m. And it's blue skies and no precipitation, so great flying conditions. You could take off anytime."

"Did you tell him I owe him a truck?" Peter asked, smiling, happy to be going home.

"It didn't come up," Mary deadpanned. "But I'm sure he'll take an IOU."

"I'm good for it," Peter said, "I guess. Hey, I left my briefcase and phone up at his place."

"He knows," Mary said. "He wants to give them to you personally. He said he had some sort of business transaction he wanted to talk to you about."

Peter cocked his head. "That's interesting," he said thoughtfully. "You could say I've got something for him as well."

"Well, isn't that special!" Jim said, grinning.

"It won't be the same here without you. It's been fun having you," Mary said.

"The two of you are absolutely amazing people," Peter said. "You saved my life. I don't know how I can repay you."

Jim shook his head. "You gave us an opportunity for love and service," he said. "From where we sit, we are equal on the exchange."

Peter sighed. He didn't know what else to say.

In the distance, the three of them could hear snowplows.

"Sounds like you're gonna get sprung quicker than we expected," Mary said.

"I'll never forget you guys as long as I live," Peter said. "You didn't just save my life. You changed it. Everything."

"As soon as the plows get done, we can run you up to Eddy's place," Mary said.

"It's hard to believe it's been only a week," Peter said. "Sometimes it just seems like a few moments, and sometimes it seems like forever. Anyway, I would love that ride."

"Shall we? You'll be on your way, so you probably don't want to waste a minute with us any longer."

"I love you guys," Peter said, "but you're right, I'm ready to go home."

29

HOMEBOUND

JIM AND MARY ESCORTED PETER TO THE GARAGE, and they all loaded into the Land Rover, then drove up the hill that led toward Eddy's home. When they reached the point where the truck had tumbled off the highway into the canyon, they paused. Peter realized again how blessed he was that God had spared him.

They drove in silence for the next forty minutes. The day was beautiful, the sky a cloudless robin's egg blue, with sunlight reflecting off fresh snow in every direction. The mountains of the region were all capped with snow and glinted in the sunshine.

They continued in silence until they reached the gates that surrounded Eddy's compound. Someone was watching on a security camera. The gates swung open, and as Jim pulled up to the portico, Eddy came out of the house and ran toward the car.

No butler this time. Instead, Eddy himself opened the door for Peter while Jim and Mary waited in the car.

"Peter!" Eddy exclaimed, patting Peter on the shoulder as he escorted him into the great hall of the mammoth chalet. "You're in one piece! We were so scared, and I felt so responsible!"

Peter reached for the edge of a table to steady himself and shook his head. "You had nothing to do with it," he said. "It was just my stubbornness. I should've stayed. In fact, I probably should've just stayed in Dallas!"

Eddy took Peter's arm and led him to a chair in the living room, the same room where Peter had met a clutch of investment bankers just a week ago. That seemed like a lifetime ago now.

The house was perfectly still. Peter sat down, grateful for the assistance, and relaxed back into the chair. Even that short walk was a huge amount of effort for Peter at this stage in his recovery.

"I've got your briefcase," Eddy said. "It's right over here. And your phone."

He brought the briefcase over to Peter, who stared at it as if it were a long-lost friend.

"I think you might be ready for an upgrade to your bag," Eddy said in a slightly teasing tone.

"What I used to consider to be a good luck charm, I now see as a blessing," Peter said. "It's my messenger bag. It always has been."

"All right. Whatever," Eddy said, slightly puzzled. "It better hold a pretty good message. I don't know who's gonna buy a house from you with an old bag like that!"

"Where's Trish?" Peter asked.

At the mention of his wife, Eddy shook his head and looked down.

"She's in Aspen, scouting locations for the new house with your boy Digby," Eddy said. "I think she might be auditioning to be Digby's wife number four. Know what I mean?"

Peter laughed but caught himself. "I'm sorry," he said quickly. "I know she's your wife. But she would actually be number five, if you're keeping score."

"I feel terrible about how the whole thing turned out," Eddy said, "especially with you having that accident and everything."

Peter shook his head firmly. "That's what I want to talk to you about. Eddy, will you forgive me?"

"Forgive you? For what?"

"I would like to ask your forgiveness for being unprofessional. It's your right to choose who you want to build your house. I insulted your wife. I judged you for being rich and insensitive. I did it behind your back. I owe you an apology. Please forgive me."

"You are forgiven, ol' chap," Eddy said in his mock British accent, revealing his discomfort with the level of genuineness and authenticity Peter was offering.

"Thank you for that, Eddy."

Eddy cleared his throat. "How was your week?" he asked.

"Well, it was the best and worst thing that ever happened to me. I met these amazing people. They rescued me and took me in. I had an encounter with God or, at least, with two of His angels." He paused for a moment.

Eddy stroked his chin. "I've never met any angels," he said thoughtfully. "Of course, I'm a hedge fund guy—not exactly angel territory."

"There *is* such thing as an angel investor," Peter said. "What I know for sure is that God invested in me this entire week."

"I had a lot of time to think," Peter began, "lying on my back, basically immobilized and wondering if I'd ever be able to walk or move again. Fortunately, things seem to be moving in the right direction, but it was touch and go, I tell you that."

Eddy nodded. "So what grand thoughts did you have while you were hanging out with your angel buddies?"

"I think I found my calling in life," Peter said. "You could say . . . I fell into it. When I went over the cliff. By the way, I owe you a truck."

Eddy shook his head quickly. "Don't be silly," he said. "I'm just glad you're alive."

"I want to work for a particular type of client. We can talk more about it later, but I feel really clear about who I am called to serve through my business."

"Well, you are so good at what you do. It would be a waste to not have you maximize the talents God gave you," Eddy offered, seeming uncomfortable with the religious talk but trying to humor Peter.

"Eddy, you might just be one of the good guys."

Eddy grinned. "Keep that to yourself," he said. "If word got out in my industry, I'd be toast!"

Both men laughed.

"Your secret's safe with me," Peter said.

"Hey, we're keeping those nice folks waiting. Let's let them get you to the airport. The jet's standing by. I'm just so happy everything turned out okay."

"I agree," Peter said.

Under his own steam, Peter carefully lifted himself out of the chair and picked up his beloved briefcase, which he viewed in a whole new light.

"Thank you for everything," he said to Eddy.

"Here, let me get you to the door," Eddy said. Eddy took Peter's arm and walked him through the hallway to the front door, stopping at the hall closet, where the butler had stashed Peter's coat.

"You'll probably want this," Eddy said.

"No, thanks. That's an old wineskin," Peter said.

Eddy seemed puzzled.

The two men shook hands again, and Eddy led Peter out the front door.

To Peter's surprise, Mary and Jim were gone. *As it should be*, he thought. *Selfless servants on to the next adventure.*

"I'm happy for you, ol' Pete from Mesquite."

Peter's eyes widened. He normally bristled when someone else called him that. Not today.

Behave! echoed in his head again, but with a different meaning now.

*Peter, when you rest in who I made you to **be**, you will **have** all that I am calling you to do. I have plans for you. Just listen, and answer the call. Behave!*

Finally. Peter was on his way home.

The End

ABOUT
THE AUTHOR

ROBIN POU is an executive coach, author, and founder of a leadership development firm.

Robin started his career as an attorney before shifting to the business world where he became a successful entrepreneur who founded three companies and oversaw their growth by serving as chief operating officer. Robin currently serves as a chief advisor and strategist to the top leaders of numerous nonprofit organizations, each of whom is a pioneer leader in their vertical.

As an executive coach and frequent keynote speaker, Robin works with Fortune 500 executives and CEOs of high-growth organizations. His clients have included GM Financial, Time Warner, the Match Group, the *Dallas Morning News*, and Sotheby's.

Robin's insights as an established leadership expert have been featured in leading media publications including *Bloomberg*, *Forbes*, and the Associated Press. Robin is also a contributor to the *Dallas Morning News*, and he also shares his latest leadership insights in a popular weekly newsletter called *The Confident Leader*.

Robin also created the *Leadership Doubt Index*—a pioneering workplace survey of top leaders that reveals significant implications on how successful leaders frequently question a critical aspect of their leadership. As part of this work, Robin founded *National Confident Leader Week*, which is an annual, nationwide initiative that aims to enhance leadership effectiveness by better understanding how leaders question their abilities, manage their doubt, and then ultimately cope with those experiences.

Robin's previous book, *Performance Intelligence at Work,* which he cowrote with sports psychologist Julie Bell, brings the principles of sport psychology to the business arena. Industry leaders can leverage these principles to defeat leadership doubt, gain greater confidence, and achieve peak performance.

Robin lives in Dallas, Texas, with his wife, Karen, and their three kiddos: Robert, Cate, and Boyd.